C000164969

WELCOME TO MOONSHINE

The Daydreamer Chronicles: Book 2

Jethro Punter

Copyright © 2018 Jethro Punter

All rights reserved

The characters and events portrayed in this book are fictitious. Any similarity
to real persons, living or dead, is coincidental and not intended by the author.

No part of this book may be reproduced, or stored in a retrieval system,
or transmitted in any form or by any means, electronic, mechanical,
photocopying, recording, or otherwise, without express written permission
of the publisher.

ISBN-13: 9781980782735
ISBN-10: 1980782733

V_04_01_21
email:jpunterwrites@gmail.com

To anyone who read the first book (this probably means you)
With special thanks to Chris B for all his help with the edits
and with extra special thanks to my Wife (for managing
to somehow put up with me during the last year...)

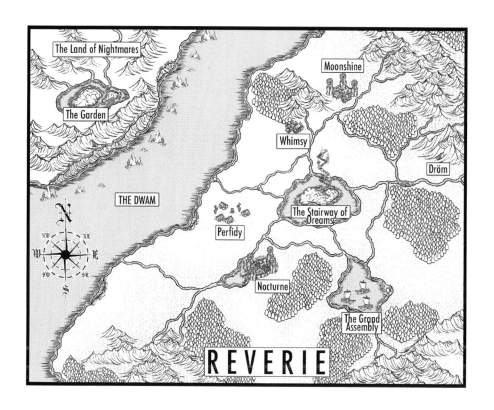

PROLOGUE

'Flapjack' Johnson was running. He was finding the experience less than enjoyable, it having been a very long time since he had last tried it. The bulkiness of his body, which most of the time he found to be useful, and which other people generally found intimidating, was definitely working against him now. Already he could feel a sharp pain in his side, the early start of a stitch that he knew was only going to get worse, but the discomfort didn't stop him, if anything it spurred him to go even faster. He was pretty certain that the pain he was experiencing as a result of running was a lot less than that he could expect if he dared stop.

"Typical," he thought to himself bitterly as he skidded around a corner, heavy flat feet struggling to gain traction on the damp floor. Moonshine had been a new start for him, the place was weird, true enough, but as a result the other residents didn't seem that fussy about who lived there. For him that had been enough. He wasn't entirely sure where, or even why, he had originally picked up the rather unpleasant nickname 'Flapjack', but it certainly wasn't due to his good manners or friendly nature. He had burned all his bridges in Nocturne and most of the other major cities of Reverie some time ago, having sunk inevitably to the very bottom of the criminal underworld in each of them, one after the other.

As a result, Moonshine had been the only place left for him to try and carve out some sort of future. He had heard of its reputation as a haven for all sorts of strange individuals and troubled souls and sure enough, it had welcomed him with open arms a few weeks ago. Almost immediately he had found a place to live, somewhere that had met his two main (and only) criteria of being both cheap and available. Within two more days he had found a job that suited his abilities pretty well, working night shift security for a company that, despite only recently moving into the area, now seemed to be employing pretty much half the population of Moonshine. However, amongst all the apparent good luck, which should have set off mental alarm bells straight away, as life had taught him early on that his wasn't a charmed existence, the job had turned out to be a mistake, a really big one.

"It's not fair," his panicking mind shouted at him as he ran, as if that was any help. It wasn't his fault... it had just been a series of really bad coincidences, to have been on night shift tonight, to have failed to pay full attention to his route, to have taken a wrong turn, and to have seen.... His mind recoiled from the memory, much too terrible to dwell upon for even a moment, and instead pulled him back to the present, despite desperately not wanting to be there either. As it did so he barged through the last door that led out the back of the building and onto the cobbled street. The cold of the night air hit him hard in the face, making his eyes water after the muggy atmosphere of the factory. He paused for a moment to see if he could hear any sound of pursuit in the corridor behind him, any footsteps. Breathing heavily he leant with his arm resting against the nearest wall, but there seemed to be nothing above the sound of his own rasping breath, just the empty darkness.

Allowing himself a brief exhalation of relief he started to walk away from the building, trying to look as calm and natural as he could manage. It was only then, as he walked just beyond the glow of the nearest lantern that he heard it. A gentle jingling noise just behind him, musical and cheery, sounding almost like Christmas bells. He spun around, certain that there had been nothing behind him only the moment before, and for a very, very brief moment Flapjack Johnson cursed his run of bad luck one final time.

CHAPTER 1

Grimble wiggled his toes and immediately winced in discomfort as a riot of pins and needles began to work its way angrily from the end of his foot to his heavily bandaged ankle. His left leg, the source of his current problems, was raised in front of him, with his foot resting on a pile of carefully stacked cushions, stubby blunt toes sticking out from the end of his dressing. Until he had tried moving, the whole arrangement had felt remarkably (and surprisingly) comfortable. As a result, every now and then he would let this feeling overrule his natural pessimism and try some slight movement, always with the same painful result. Letting the pain in his leg subside, he concentrated instead on the glow of warm sunlight on his face, enjoying the swell of wellbeing it brought with it, pulling his attention back away from the lingering injury.

For the last three weeks he had slowly been recuperating, splitting his time between a comfortable bed inside the little townhouse and an equally comfortable chair out in the small, paved garden area. He thought back to the clash that had caused his injury and shuddered slightly, still troubled by the memories that sprung unwanted to the forefront of his mind. The brief, tumultuous battle with the Nightmares had nearly cost him his leg, but to his surprise and secret gratitude, Lucid had come to his aid just in time, turning what could have been a fatal moment into one which was merely extremely uncomfortable.

He sighed heavily, owing Lucid was going to be nearly as painful as any of the physical injuries he had picked up ... and much, much more annoying. Still, he thought to himself, despite his insistence that he wanted to be left in peace to recover,

Lucid had visited him every single day, loping in on his ridiculously long legs, placing his stupidly tall hat on the table and making idiotic, pointless small talk in his incredibly frustrating accent. At this thought Grimble stared back across the yard, through the open window and at the clock slowly marking the passing of time on the kitchen wall. As he thought, there was still more than an hour until Lucid was expected to turn up again and he was getting increasingly impatient for the chance to be annoyed at him once again. Turning back to face the brick wall of the yard he shuffled down slightly in his seat to find a comfortable resting position and closed his eyes, deciding the best way to pass the time until Lucid's arrival was with a quick snooze.

He was just starting to doze off when he was disturbed by a noise from across the yard's wall. It was a high warbling laugh, sprinkled liberally throughout with individual notes of humour and warmth, a laugh that was completely infectious and impossible to hear without smiling. Not seeming to be aware of this fact, or if he was aware, simply not caring, rather than smiling Grimble's scowl deepened and he slouched down further in his seat.

There was a pause in the laughter, a moment of silence and then a loud and unexpected belching noise, reverberating around the yard so violently it shook Grimble's teeth. When this settled he could hear the laughter again, moving away into the distance. Then there was another pause, a sound which could only be described as something like a cat playing the drums while falling down the stairs, then more laughter and finally a series of strange parping noises. As the last set of sounds faded the odd cacophony moved too far away for Grimble to hear any more details.

"Oh for goodness sake," Grimble muttered to himself miserably, any momentary relaxation or pleasure completely forgotten. "That's the last thing I need, on top of everything else, whatever is she doing here?"

CHAPTER 2

Back in what he supposed he would still refer to as the 'real' world, despite the lines between the two having become increasingly blurred, Adam was having a bad day... although it was perhaps not as bad as some he had recently had. He wasn't, for example, having to escape from pursuing nightmare monsters or save the world, but it was still quite bad enough.

"I don't see the point of this," he grumbled to Charlie, his best friend and currently also his reluctant homework buddy. "I really don't care what 'x' is equal to." Looking down at the page in front of him the numbers and letters seemed to dance around the paper, hiding behind each other, pulling faces and generally mocking him and his inability to make any sense of them.

"Perhaps we should have a break for a bit," Charlie replied, even his relatively deep reserves of natural patience running short after more than an hour spent failing to help Adam achieve even a basic level of algebraic understanding. "Why don't we go and do something else for a while and then come back to it when your head's had a chance to clear?"

Adam nodded gratefully, more than happy to escape from the textbooks for a while. It was the weekend after all, and it seemed a terrible waste to spend it all with his head stuck in school books when he could be doing any number of more exciting things. He was also feeling pretty tired, which he knew was his own fault, having spent most of his nights recently in the dream world, or more simply 'Reverie' as it seemed to be known by its odd inhabitants. As he stood up from the table his hand went unconsciously to the pendant that hung around his neck, which had recently once again become his means of entering

Reverie when he slept at night. Adam was convinced that the pendant held more secrets, but unfortunately that was the big problem with mysteries, you didn't really know what they were until they revealed themselves. So for the moment he just satisfied himself with keeping the pendant with him at all times, with the hope that eventually he would find out more.

Charlie also stood up, stretching as he did so and taking the opportunity to push his dark brown hair away from his eyes. This week's hairstyle featured a long fringe at the front, with a strange selection of spikes and tufts towards the back of his head, which Charlie thought made him look like the hero in his favourite Manga cartoon. Adam thought it made the top of Charlie's head look a bit like a duck's bottom, but hadn't had the heart to tell him that... yet.

Taking a break from their homework, the two boys strolled out into the garden of Charlie's house, enjoying the open space, the fresh air and the complete absence of maths questions. Charlie had a quick look around to make sure that no one else was within earshot. "So what happened last night?" he asked, his eyes wide.

Adam shrugged in reply. "Nothing much, when I fell asleep here I woke up back in Reverie. I met Lucid again, same as the night before, we trained for a while and he let me know how things were going."

Charlie nodded enthusiastically, "and?" he prompted.

"Same as before really," Adam replied. "Waking Nora up seems to have solved things in Reverie, for the moment at least."

The mention of Nora brought up some further uncomfortable thoughts. Since her return to school Adam had the strong feeling that Nora remembered more about her time in Reverie than she was letting on. Several times he had caught her staring at him with an odd expression on her face, but despite this, they hadn't exchanged more than a couple of words since she had rejoined his class. There had however been a number of slightly embarrassed smiles whenever they saw each other or made eye contact across the classroom. While Adam desperately wanted to know if Nora did remember anything, it wasn't exactly an easy conversation to start. How could you ask someone you hardly knew; "Do you remember me rescuing you from a giant evil nightmare?" without sounding very, very weird.

"And still no news on your Mum?" Charlie asked, concern taking the place of the previous excitement and interest in his voice.

"Not yet," Adam admitted, "but it hasn't been that long since things settled down there… and Lucid has promised that he and Grimble will help me look for her as soon as they are able to."

A raindrop spattered off Adam's nose, catching him by surprise and cutting short his conversation. While they had been chatting clouds had gathered overhead and taken the place of the previously pleasant sunlight. As more rain began to fall, the boys went back inside to have another go at the algebra homework, the darkening sky reflecting Adam's feelings about the whole thing perfectly.

Several painful hours later and they had finally finished the last of the homework, Charlie having eventually become so frustrated that he had completed the last two questions on Adam's behalf. His grumpy explanation for how he had worked out the last answer, "that's just what it is…" lacked something in Adam's opinion, but he couldn't be bothered to do any more either, so he shut the textbook in relief instead of complaining.

They decided to spend what was left of the afternoon down at the local Library, Charlie having recently developed a heroically hopeless crush on the Trainee Librarian. As a result, the two boys had already spent most of their spare time the previous day there. Adam had caught up on the latest comics and picked up a couple of fantasy books to read, while Charlie had spent most of his time strutting up and down the aisles of books like a slightly scruffy peacock, trying without any success to get the Trainee's attention. Although he secretly felt the whole thing was pointless, Adam had still helped out where he could, laughing uproariously every time Charlie said anything, funny or not. This hadn't really seemed to do any good, but had drawn a lot of disapproving looks from the other customers and a stern shushing from the Head Librarian.

As they made their way back in, the Head Librarian was once again manning the front desk, acknowledging their return with a relatively friendly nod. Adam and Charlie returned the nod with a polite "hello," while remembering that it had only been a matter of weeks since the same man had been chasing them down the street intent on attacking them both. Admittedly he hadn't quite been himself, having temporarily been possessed by one of the very worst residents of the dream world, a particularly unpleasant type of Nightmare known as an 'Incubo'. As a result, while Adam was fairly sure that the Librarian didn't have any memories of the event, it still felt strange to now be exchanging harmless pleasantries.

✳ ✳ ✳

At breakfast the following morning Charlie seemed more subdued than normal. Generally, by the time Adam got downstairs and joined him, Charlie would be halfway through his pre-breakfast toast, which he claimed he needed to give him the energy boost he needed to then eat his main breakfast. But when Adam got into the kitchen Charlie was sat idly pushing his cereal around in its bowl, his expression miserable.

"Everything all right?" Adam asked him as he poured his own cereal.

"What?" Charlie looked up for a moment with large dark circles under his eyes. "Oh…fine, I'm fine, just slept a bit badly that's all."

He was also unusually quiet on the walk into school. Most mornings the journey gave them the chance to talk over the events taking place in Reverie without the risk of being overheard, but today Charlie seemed to be the one in his own world, replying to Adam's questions with terse one-word answers and then clamming up again. He had his hands thrust deep into his coat pockets and his hood raised despite the warm weather as if he was deliberately trying to shut out the rest of the world. After a few more unsuccessful attempts to start a conversation Adam decided to leave Charlie to his thoughts and ended up trailing, rather despondently, a few steps behind him instead.

By lunchtime Adam found himself once again serving a detention with Miss Grudge, having not quite managed to keep his concentration focused during geography. Despite his best efforts his mind had kept drifting back to his time in Reverie. Although things had calmed down since he and his companions had stopped the Horror, there was a lot he felt he still needed to catch up on. Lucid had told him that Henry had recently retired from the Five, the battle with the Nightmares having convinced him that his place was firmly in the Library, where he felt most comfortable and more importantly, far less likely to be attacked by rampaging monsters.

So far a replacement hadn't been found, so along with the disappearance of the Lady and Maya during the last incursion of the Horror, the Five was currently down to a very limited 'Two'. However Lucid seemed confident that their numbers would be back to full strength soon enough. Most of all though he wanted to see how Grimble was doing. The last time he had visited the dream world Lucid had reassured Adam that Grimble was recovering well, but currently refusing to see visitors. For Adam the frustration this caused was two-fold. Despite Grimble's uncompromisingly grumpy nature, they had shared an amazing adventure together and over time Adam had grown to think of him as a friend. A difficult friend, one that was constantly critical, that would complain and grumble at every opportunity, but a friend all the same. The fact that he hadn't seen Grimble since their battle with Isenbard and the Horror was therefore playing on his mind.

The second part of his frustration stemmed from the fact that both Grimble and Lucid had promised to help him look for his mother, who he now firmly believed to be somewhere within Reverie. Until Grimble had recovered it seemed unlikely that they could start their search. He was so deeply engrossed in these thoughts that he had been caught completely off balance when Miss Grudge had asked Adam what the chief export of Mexico was. He had replied "Grimble" without thinking, resulting in most of the class laughing at him. It had also led to his current detention.

Miss Grudge was sat behind her desk, reading a self-improvement book of some kind, as she did nearly every detention session. The type of book that had a title full of brittle optimism like, 'How to mindfully think your way to inner satisfaction and utter contentment in seventeen easy steps.' Over his many detention sessions Adam had seen Miss Grudge read any number of similar books, none of which seemed to have given her the answer she was looking for. Each one of them was eventually consigned to the bin and replaced with another even more optimistically titled volume, promising even better results. Seeing her read these books day after day made Adam feel surprisingly sorry for her, despite their rather strained relationship. Still, for the moment, the latest book had her completely engrossed, so Adam was able to risk looking away from his work for a minute. He glanced out the window to see what a normal, non-detention, lunchbreak looked like.

The field outside was filled with normal playground activities, clusters of kids chatting and playing, posing and gossiping. Out of the corner of his eye he caught sight of Charlie, stood on his own, leant against a wall and still looking pretty sorry for himself. He watched as Charlie reached into his bag and pulled out his packed lunch, looking at it sadly for a moment before dropping it straight into the rubbish. Adam stared for a moment in amazement. Not wanting all his breakfast was one thing, but Charlie must really be feeling bad not to eat his lunch, it was literally unheard of. Charlie was famous for his appetite. Adam could still remember the last time they had gone together to an 'all you can eat' buffet, where Charlie had made a spirited, although eventually doomed, attempt to put the place out of business. There was a meaningful cough from Miss Grudge's direction and Adam quickly looked back down at his work, trying his best to give off an impression of studious concentration.

It wasn't until they walked home after school that Adam had the chance to properly ask Charlie how he was feeling. Even from his position a couple of steps behind him Adam could tell that Charlie wasn't his normal self. It might have just been a trick of the light, but it looked like even the back of his ears had a rather unhealthy green tinge to them. It took him a little while to open up to Adam's persistent questioning, but eventually Charlie admitted just how bad he was feeling.

"Okay," he conceded "I feel rotten, alright...really, really rotten," grimacing as he said it.

"Maybe you should have stayed at home if you felt that ill?" asked Adam, worried by the unusual depth of misery in his friend's voice.

"I didn't think it would last all day," Charlie shrugged. "I woke up feeling rubbish but thought it would probably wear off."

Stopping for a moment he let his shoulders slump back down, relaxing slightly from their previous rigid, defensive position. "What I am going to say might sound a bit strange... but I suppose if anyone is going to understand strange it's probably you." Adam nodded, he couldn't really disagree with that, not after everything he had told Charlie about the dream world. If anything he was now an expert in strangeness. "Last night I had a really odd dream," Charlie continued. "Like...really strange. Nothing made any sense and it was a relief to wake up and get out of it... but as soon as I woke up I felt really sick, like I had a fever."

He paused again, letting his embarrassment get the better of him. "Come on, let's get home. I need to sit down...or lie down," he said rather shortly, his shoulders hunching once again as he turned away. Without pausing to see if Adam had anything further to say Charlie stalked off down the street, discouraging any further conversation.

Once they got back to his house, after a few minutes spent

sitting miserably in the corner of the living room Charlie had excused himself and spent the rest of the evening shut in his room, leaving Adam in slightly awkward conversation with Charlie's parents instead. While he had now lived with them for several weeks, and they had been nothing but welcoming in every possible way, he still felt a bit like an intruder and with Charlie locked away from the rest of the family he felt it more than ever. It was therefore with a feeling of slightly guilty relief that he finally escaped upstairs to the guest room, which he was slowly learning to think of as his. As with the previous few nights, when he eventually fell asleep, he was clutching the pendant tightly in his hand, keen to re-enter the dream world.

CHAPTER 3

As seemed to have now become his habit, Lucid was lounging comfortably at the edge of the clearing where Adam arrived in Reverie, springing to his feet enthusiastically when he spotted him.

"Good news!" he said, seeming to be in a particularly buoyant mood, even by his shockingly cheerful standards. "I visited Grimble earlier today and he is sufficiently recovered to move back to the mansion. He is also apparently ready to receive visitors. I know you have been looking forward to seeing him..." he paused and then added with a sly grin "...although I honestly don't know why."

"Does that mean that we can start to look for my mum?" Adam asked, not able to hold back the question any longer.

"I believe we can," Lucid replied, although Adam could see that he looked slightly troubled as he said it. "But there is also something else that we need to discuss with you. It seems your fame has spread, you have a visitor."

Despite his initial disappointment that meeting this visitor would delay the long-awaited search for his mother, Adam had to admit he also felt a little intrigued. Lucid filled him in on the details as they walked across the city. It seemed that someone had travelled across from one of the furthest corners of Reverie to see Adam, from an area known as 'Moonshine'. From the face Lucid pulled as he said the name, Adam could tell that Moonshine was both out of the ordinary and apparently not somewhere that Lucid thought very highly of.

Instead of the normal route they tended to walk, taking them to the mansion that Adam had come to know as the main meeting place of the Five, Lucid took a side road off the Market Square. The houses down this smaller street were pressed snugly against each other. They weren't exactly a terrace, with each one being built separate from its neighbours, but they were so tightly spaced you would struggle to fit more than a single finger's width between them. The walls were also slightly uneven, so in many places the houses were touching, leaning against each other for support. Looking ahead Adam could see that the fronts of the houses had been painted in a range of contrasting colours, reds, blues and yellows, giving the whole street an infectiously cheerful look. Turning to Lucid, Adam shared his surprise that Grimble, with his dour tastes, would choose to live in such a place.

"Aha…" Lucid replied with a twinkle in his eye. "What is it you say in your world….Don't judge a book by its cover?"

Adam nodded, although he often did judge books on that exact basis, having a particular weakness for cover art featuring mysterious cloaked figures and big gold writing, or anything with a dragon on it, (or best of all a mysterious cloaked figure riding a dragon completely surrounded by gold writing).

"There is more to Grimble than it appears." Lucid leant in towards Adam conspiratorially. "In fact, there is even a rumour that on one occasion…" Adam's eyes widened and he held his breath, waiting to hear what Lucid was going to share. "…he was seen smiling." Lucid gave a broad wink in response to Adam's groan, then continued down the street before stopping at a particularly quaint house painted in a pleasant shade of cornflower blue. Lucid knocked a couple of times on the low wooden door, before pulling a large iron key from his pocket and letting himself in, ducking under the crooked doorframe.

"Hello!" Lucid called out as he made his way firstly through the snug-looking living room and then a compact kitchen. An increasingly bemused Adam trailed along behind him, fairly sure he had just seen a kitten patterned tea-towel hanging neatly from a hook to one side of the oven.

"Grimble really lives here?" he asked Lucid, unable to keep

the tone of disbelief from his voice.

Lucid looked back over his shoulder, a quizzical eyebrow raised. "Surely it's not so hard to believe?" he asked, before calling out "Hello!" again. There was a pause and then Adam heard Grimble reply.

"I'm out here, in the garden....like every other time you have visited me, you lanky buffoon." Adam breathed a sigh of relief, it was good to see that some things hadn't changed.

Grimble was painstakingly making his way to his feet when Adam and Lucid entered the yard, it was clear that he was still in some discomfort as he awkwardly placed a crutch under his right arm to steady himself before turning to face them both.

"Welcome back Adam," Grimble greeted him gruffly, not exactly smiling but with less of a scowl on his face than normal, which Adam presumed meant he was pleased to see him.

"How are you?" Adam asked, his gaze dropping to his heavily bandaged leg.

"Fine," Grimble replied. "Fortunately we Drömer are made of sterner stuff than you squishy humans; it would take more than a few Nightmares to put me down."

"Exactly," added Lucid, grinning affectionately at his shorter friend. "I am sure you will be dancing the night away again before long."

"Idiot," Grimble grunted, before turning his attention back to Adam.

"I presume that Lucid has informed you about our visitor?" he asked.

"Yes... or at least he has told me a little bit, but I don't know anything about them other than they come from a place called Moonshine," Adam replied, noticing Grimble's scowl deepen.

"That's correct; your visitor is from the edge of the Great Dream. She's one of... them," said Grimble, his face still thunderous. "Even worse than that, she's the Queen... if such a place can have a Queen."

"What do you mean, one of them?" asked Adam, surprised by Grimble's scathing tone.

"Do you remember any of your strangest dreams?" Grimble replied, eyes narrowing. "Not just the averagely odd ones, but the really incomprehensible dreams where nothing made any kind of sense. The kind of dream you get if you ate too much cheese straight before bed and were grateful to wake up before you went quite mad."

"I suppose…" Adam began.

"Well that's where 'they' come from," Grimble continued angrily, without waiting for Adam to finish. "'They' live in a corner of this world where all the oddest dreams happen." He paused for a moment, seeming to get caught up in a distant memory, then adding with a shudder. "I have been there once and I am never, ever going again!"

"So what's so bad about the people who live there exactly?" Adam asked him, still a little confused by how strongly Grimble seemed to feel about the matter. "Are they evil?"

"No… not exactly evil," Grimble conceded reluctantly. "But they are very, very strange and the whole place is… extremely disorganised." From the way he said the word 'disorganised' it was clear that this was at least as bad as 'evil' in Grimble's view, perhaps worse.

"The Queen that Grimble refers to… she's been looking for you," Lucid added in a much more measured tone. "Apparently word of a new Daydreamer has made its way as far as Moonshine and the Queen seems to think there is something that you can help her with."

"We have arranged to meet her at the mansion later today." Grimble gestured to the gate at the back of the small yard, leading back into the city. "As it will take me a while to walk there, we should probably get underway."

The narrow alleyway behind Grimble's yard quickly gave way to wider streets and before long Adam found himself on the main road that he recognised as the route to the mansion. As they walked up the road, Grimble's uncompromising refusal to accept any help making their progress painfully slow, Adam's attention was caught by a large and unusual looking cart working its way down the street towards them. It was rumbling along on big metal bound wheels, a dark blue smoke billowing from a slightly rickety cast iron chimney to one side and a pair of glass canisters filled with a swirling pink gas hanging on the other. At the front of the cart, on a small platform high off the ground, sat a short driver sporadically squeezing the bulb of a brass horn to warn of his approach. He was wearing soot-stained blue overalls and some heavy looking brass goggles to protect his eyes from the smoke, which swirled persistently around his face.

As the cart reached them the driver pulled on a long metal handbrake sticking up between the two seats and the cart shuddered to a temporary halt, the driver parping the hooter while scowling pointedly at Adam and his two companions. It took a minute for Grimble to hobble his way to the side of the road, by which time the cart was shuddering violently, smoke gushing from the chimney at an alarming rate. Wiping condensation from his goggles with a finger of his heavily gloved hand the driver released the brake with a look of relief and the cart rattled its way off up the road.

As it passed them Adam could see a symbol was painted on the side of the cart, a large creature with the head of a lion, a second goat-like head and a long snaking tail, all inscribed neatly within a golden circle, the initials C.R.H.C emblazoned in bold print underneath.

"Bah, if that's progress you can keep it," Grimble muttered angrily to himself as the cart rumbled noisily away, then spat contemptuously onto the street.

"What was that exactly?" Adam asked, not having seen anything quite like it in Reverie up until now.

"The Chimera Reverie Holding Company." Lucid's voice sounded unusually bitter. "Popped up out of nowhere about a year ago and now their technology can be found all over the place." He grimaced as he continued. "That was one of their Effluvium Carts, apparently we will all be using them to transport goods in the future."

Hearing that Adam could understand Lucid's concern. His people, the Sornette, currently made their living by carrying and trading goods by barge across the Weave, the river of dreams that ran through the land. The delivery cart that had just passed them could, he supposed, be an unwelcome threat to that long-established way of life.

"I thought I recognised the image on the side of the cart," Adam said, having recently studied Greek mythology at school, with some of the more interesting facts having stayed in his head. "That was a Chimera?"

"Yes, it's the logo they use on most of their business interests, you will probably see that image quite a bit if you look out for it," Grimble informed him. "They seem to have their meddling fingers all over the place, transport, businesses and restaurants. You name it and five minutes later they will have bought it, supposedly improved it and sold it back to you at twice the price."

"And it has become a lot worse in the last few weeks," added Lucid. "Until recently you would just see them now and then, but all of a sudden you can't seem to go more than a few steps without running into something with their name on it, under it or hidden somewhere behind it."

Adam kept his eyes peeled as they finished the walk back to the mansion, and sure enough on two further occasions he spotted the Chimera symbol. The first time on a stack of crates outside one of the street side cafés and the second on a hoarding outside one of the larger buildings they passed as they drew close to their destination. Although he knew it was his imagination, as he continued down the street, he was convinced that he could feel the eyes of the Chimera burning into the back of his head as he walked away.

CHAPTER 4

It was with a feeling of pleasant familiarity that Adam walked down the pathway to the grand old house, Lucid slightly ahead and Grimble limping a few places behind. The heavy front door no longer felt as imposing as it had when he had first visited, especially when it was opened by the slightly breathless and pink-cheeked Mrs. Snugs, who had very obviously just ran, (or at the very least bustled at speed), across the mansion to answer the door to them. She smiled in unconcealed delight upon seeing Adam, embarrassing him with an enthusiastic hug.

"Ooooh welcome back Adam," she said. "I wondered when I would see you again. Mr. Lucid said you had been back in Reverie for a while." Tilting her head to one side and looking past Adam she spotted Grimble, who was lingering in the background, trying to be particularly unobtrusive. Unfortunately for him, this was proving difficult as every step he took resulted in the tap of his crutch on the stone slabs of the hallway.

"Mr. Grimble!" she gushed in delight, "so good to see you up and about," and she stepped forward with her arms outstretched, offering another hug. Grimble's rather awkward attempt to avoid her caused him to stumble back, tripping over his own crutch and landing with a painful sounding bump on the ground. Despite the uncomfortable looking tumble, Adam suspected that he still preferred this to the offered embrace.

They managed to make it to the main dining room without any further incidents (of either affection or injury) and Mrs. Snugs bustled off to arrange for some drinks and nibbles, looking particularly excited by the combination of Adam and Grimble's return and the prospect of a royal visit. Lucid had tried explaining that the 'Queen' of Moonshine wasn't royalty in the normal sense, but that hadn't reduced Mrs. Snug's enthusiasm in the slightest.

Lucid, Grimble and Adam took the chance to sit for a few minutes while they waited for their guest's arrival, giving Grimble the opportunity to regain his breath, the walk across the city having taken more out of him than he seemed willing to openly admit. Adam was about to use this chance to raise the question of the search for his mother again, when there was a polite cough and a knock at the door. This was followed by Mrs. Snugs opening the door and backing in, walking in a type of awkward, hunched, half curtsy.

"Your guest is here gentlemen," she informed them, pulling the second of the double doors open and then walking back out of the room, still bobbing up and down and looking extremely flustered.

The sound entered the room a few seconds before their guest did, a pleasant bubbling laugh. It was pure and almost child-like, taking innocent joy in the sheer act of laughter. This initial warm impression was however rather spoiled by the weird and very loud clanging noise which followed immediately after. There was then a brief pause before Adam heard a deeply un-pleasant and flatulent parping sound almost directly outside the door. Looking at his companions Adam could see that Lucid looked largely unconcerned, whereas Grimble had gone white in the face with fear, disgust or some other scarcely contained emotion.

Before Adam could fully recover from this sudden and very odd assault on his ears, a small figure walked into the room, accompanied by two outlandishly dressed courtiers. Both of the courtiers appeared to be Drömer, the same race as Grimble, although their dress was the complete opposite of his dour appearance. They were wearing extremely garish clothing with their facial hair teased into braids, tied with brightly coloured bows. One of them was bowing and scraping every few seconds, with the time in between bows and scrapes spent throwing handfuls of strongly scented flower petals into the air. The other waved a miniature flag in small circles and sporadically shouted "hooray" with apparent enthusiasm.

While Adam stared on in perplexed amazement the slightly more extravagantly dressed courtier of the two paused his flag waving for a moment and pulled out a small tin trumpet, blowing a short and very discordant fanfare. "All rise for the great Deliria, Queen of Moonshine."

At this Adam awkwardly climbed to his feet, completely thrown by the odd sight he was faced with. While he did this the two courtiers had shuffled their way to either side of the doorway and stood silently, heads slightly bowed, making sure that all the attention in the room was focused upon the small figure that now approached Adam.

The first impression he got of Deliria was of a motherly figure with blond frizzy hair, carefully sculpted into a winding plait that made the top of her head look like an ice cream cone, while also adding nearly a foot to her height, (which remained short even then). Her face was broad and smiling, although caked under so much thick white make-up it seemed likely that if her expression changed the carefully applied surface would immediately crack. Her clothing was similarly bright and ostentatious, with alternating layers of lace and velvet, all of which were in a variety of colours, patterns and textures so jarring that it made even the extravagantly unique dress sense of the Sornette appear conservative and dull by comparison.

The most noticeable thing however, which made everything else fade into insignificance, was the small collection of constantly changing items that were orbiting slowly around Deliria's head, apparently just hanging in the air like a ghostly version of a baby's mobile. One moment Adam spotted a small kitten, mewing quietly, the next a tin drum, tiny floating drumsticks rapping out a lively tune. Deliria impatiently flapped at them like they were bothersome flies as they made their way in front of her face, brushing them to one side for a moment before they bobbed back into place and resumed their lazy orbit.

"Greetings Daydreamer," Deliria said, her voice surprisingly soft and pleasant, a direct contrast from the more discordant sounds which seemed to be coming from the odd items that circled her. "I am so pleased to finally meet you. I have travelled for many days to reach you here, leaving my people without the light of my regal splendour." As she said this the tin drum passing around the back of her head changed shape abruptly, becoming a small crying baby wailing grumpily to itself.

Adam nodded, unsure what to say and trying to focus on Deliria's face rather than all the surrounding oddness. "Um... hello," he said, "pleased to meet you too... your um... Majesty?" He inclined his head in a bow, not really sure if it was expected of him or not.

At his bow Deliria giggled and waved her hand coquettishly, the wailing baby changing again to become a gently waving fan, which continued to circle, its orbit widening to also take in Adam. "Very gallant young man, it is good to see that someone in this room still maintains some manners." It was pretty clear that this comment wasn't fully aimed at Adam but meant instead for someone over his shoulder. Judging from the discontented grumbling noise from behind him that someone was almost certainly Grimble.

"But enough of these pleasantries," Deliria continued, "to the business that has brought me here. As I am sure your companions have told you I come from the far edges of Reverie, a great city known as Moonshine." At this the two courtiers stepped forward and blew a short fanfare on their small tin trumpets which was particularly awful, even by their low standards. Deliria tutted and wiggled her fingers at them, at which they shuffled sheepishly back to their spots by the door.

"They're very keen bless them." Deliria said, turning back to Adam, "truly terrible at their jobs, but very, very keen." She paused, re-gathering her thoughts. "Where was I... oh yes... Moonshine, something terribly strange is happening in Moonshine."

Her explanation was disturbed by a disbelieving snort from

Grimble. "Bah... when is something strange not happening there?"

"Grimble," Deliria said calmly, not seeming to be the least bit insulted by his outburst, "my discussion is with Adam here, who perhaps does not share your prejudices." For a moment the odd items circling her paused in their orbit and Adam felt that she was making a particularly hard effort to be focused, to be taken seriously.

"I meant it when I said something strange is happening. Chimera have recently set up a new factory just outside of my beautiful city and I believe that there is something... untoward about what they are doing." Her eyes had narrowed dangerously as she spoke the word Chimera and Adam thought back to the earlier discussion with Lucid and Grimble as they passed through the city.

"You mean the Chimera & Reverie Holding Company?" he asked, hoping he had remembered the name correctly.

"Exactly," Deliria replied. "I don't know precisely what they are doing, but ever since they opened their new facility unusual... uncomfortable things have been happening. I am quite sure that they are somehow related."

"And what do you want Deliria?" asked Grimble, his tone still frosty.

"I want you to come to Moonshine," she replied. "I want you to investigate, to help. Isn't that what you are supposed to do, isn't that what the Five were made for?"

CHAPTER 5

Several hours after Deliria and her strange retinue had left, Lucid and Grimble were still arguing over her request. Lucid was in favour of travelling to Moonshine as she had asked, convinced that they should put any personal feelings aside in order to do their duty and help when asked. On the other hand, Grimble seemed almost pathologically opposed to the idea and nothing that Lucid had said to him so far seemed to alter his stubborn determination not to go anywhere near the place.

Although he had been involved in the discussion to start with, and despite his feeling that Deliria had really come to ask him rather than the other two, eventually Adam became tired of the argument. Rather than listen to the continued bickering of his friends he wandered out of the dining room to clear his head and with some luck, find something to eat or drink. Lucid and Grimble were still so deeply involved in their debate Adam wasn't even sure they noticed him leave.

He had originally intended to slip away to the kitchens and see if he could grab something from all the leftover food Mrs. Snugs had optimistically prepared for their guests, but even after his numerous visits, the winding corridors of the mansion still played tricks on Adam's mind and sense of direction. Within a few minutes he was both increasingly hungry and quite lost. He was also sure he had been walking in a straight line much further than should have been possible within the mansion. When he finally reached the end of the corridor he found himself at the base of a flight of stairs he didn't recognise from any of his previous visits. The stairs themselves were wooden and looked worn and dusty with no sign of recent use. Although he was pretty sure he should turn back and find the others, Adam was tired of their arguing, so instead he headed up the dusty staircase, intrigued to see more of the mansion.

At the top of the stairs there was a rather plain, uninspiring landing, leaving Adam feeling a little disappointed, although he wasn't really sure what he had been expecting to find. Nevertheless, he decided to look around a little more, and at a whim, picked the second door down the corridor.

The room that Adam entered looked like it hadn't been used for some time, curtains drawn tight against the sun and the furniture around the edge of the room made shapeless, veiled under heavy sheets. Looking down Adam could see that the dust on the floor was sufficiently thick for him to leave slight footprints as he crossed the room. Obviously no one had been in here for some time.

Wandering to a random dust sheet, Adam lifted the edge and peered under, however all he found was a pretty normal looking wooden dresser, certainly nothing mysterious. Making his way around the room Adam looked under several more of the sheets, uncovering tables, chairs and shelves, none of which looked unusual. Achieving nothing more than making him sneeze violently as he disturbed piles of long-dormant dust. Without thinking he had been making his way in a roughly clockwise circuit of the room and had drawn close to the heavily curtained windows. Leaning against the wall next to the windows was a smaller shape, again shrouded in sheets. As he approached it he could see a sliver of light from a gap in the curtains cutting through the general gloom, illuminating motes of disturbed dust as they circled above the shape like tiny fireflies.

Adam gripped the dust sheet and lifted it to see what was concealed beneath. This time rather than furniture, he could see that it had been used to cover a pile of smaller and more random objects. A large chest was at the centre of the pile with a number of other items leaning against it. The closest of these was a large framed painting and it was this that drew Adam's attention. In the darkness it was difficult to fully make out any detail, so he lifted the painting carefully out from the pile and leant it against the wall, facing into the room. It had been painted in dark and heavy oils, making it difficult to see any features or details in the half-light, but squinting in the gloom Adam thought it looked like a group portrait, with a number of figures just about visible.

Grasping the edge of the nearest curtain Adam pulled it to one side, closing his eyes for a moment against the bright sunlight as it streamed in. The previous darkness was immediately banished, revealing the dusty dark floor as a deep, rich red wood. Then Adam looked back at the painting once again and as he did so, everything around him seemed to grind to a halt, the flying dust disturbed by the gust of air as he opened the curtain temporarily frozen in place. The details of the painting were brought into bright relief in the direct sunlight and Adam could see that it was a portrait as he had thought. More specifically it was another of the pictures that matched the others in the portrait corridor, with a group of five individuals standing together. To the rear was the unmistakable figure of Isenbard, his white blonde hair and wide confident smile bringing back unpleasant memories of their last meeting. To the left of the group was Grimble, without his current scars and with a cheerful expression on a younger looking face. To the far right was a figure that Adam initially thought was Lucid, but on closer inspection proved to be another of the Sornette, his face sharper and less genial than Adam's friend.

However, it was the two remaining figures in the centre of the painting, stood together to the front of the group that Adam found he couldn't tear his eyes away from. A young woman was stood holding hands with a slender dark-haired man, both smiling broadly. The man's dark tousled hair framed a slim face, but it was his eyes that stood out. Rather than pupils the painter had captured what seemed to be a white glow bleeding out from each eye socket. Even though the eyes were nothing more than a simple smear of paint, Adam could almost visualise the gentle flicker, sparkling and crackling with energy. But despite the oddness of the man's appearance, it was still the woman that took most of Adam's attention. Pretty and full of youthful exuberance her wide, expressive mouth and smiling eyes were hard to mistake. Although the passing of time had added a few lines to her face and dulled the shimmer of her hair, the woman was undoubtedly his mother.

Adam's breath caught in his throat as he stared, transfixed by the painting, finding himself almost choking on a mouthful of dusty air. He slowly sank to a sitting position and continued to drink in the detail of the picture, his eyes constantly straying back to his mother. While he had been concentrating on her face up until that moment it was with a nearly equivalent level of shock that he spotted a smaller detail of the painting. A thin chain hung around her neck, on the end of which was a small oval shape. Although the painter hadn't captured it in much detail Adam knew immediately that it was the same pendant that now hung securely under his t-shirt.

* * *

It seemed that Lucid and Grimble had finished their argument by the time Adam found his way back, as Lucid was now sat alone in the dining room with his chin resting on his hands. "I saw the portrait," Adam blurted out before he could stop himself, unable to think of a different way to introduce his questions and too angry to care about being diplomatic. "I saw my mother in a portrait in one of the rooms upstairs... and I saw this in it too." He paused and fished the pendant out from under his shirt, letting it spin in the light of the hanging lamp for a moment. Lucid sat upright in his seat, blinking as he was brought back from whatever time or place he had been thinking of.

For a moment it was almost as if Adam could see Lucid's brain whirring, trying to think of an answer or an explanation that would satisfy him, but then he slumped back to his former position, chin resting on his hands once again.

"I knew you would have to be told eventually... and I am sorry that we didn't tell you before," Lucid admitted, his gaze downcast, seeming to be temporarily ashamed to make eye contact.

"But why?" Adam asked, torn between whether he felt more confused or disappointed. "Why would it matter for me to know? I wanted to know more about her... and I wanted to know more about me!"

Lucid sighed, a long, deep exhalation of breath that he seemed to use to try and clear his head before starting his explanation afresh. "It's complicated," he began, "as so many secrets are when you finally come to try and explain them. Your mother was... is a Daydreamer of incredible ability and used to be a regular visitor to Reverie." He smiled for a moment. "She ended up spending more time in this world than her own." Adam felt a slight twinge of guilt at this, realising that the same could probably now be said of him. "This might be best explained with the painting in front of us." Lucid added. "Come with me."

A few minutes later and they were back in the dusty room. Lucid paused for a moment before walking across to the painting, crouching down slightly and pointing a long finger at the man stood holding his mother's hand. "I know you believe that this is all about your mother..." Lucid said "...and I can understand why you would think that, it is all you have ever known. But there is something much more than that, something far more difficult."

Adam looked down at the painting as Lucid continued his hesitant explanation, eyes moving back and forth between the image of his mother and the man with the strangely glowing eyes who stood alongside her. "Your mother was young and... impetuous, she joined with the Five as soon as it was felt she was old enough to make that judgement. At the time that she joined, the others in the group were Grimble and Isenbard, as you no doubt already recognise. There was also my predecessor, Spindle and one other, Hugo."

Lucid paused once again and turned back to Adam. "Hugo was another dream being, very similar to the Lady. While he looked very much like any other human his real nature was always clear in his eyes, as I think the portrait captured pretty well. He was exciting, completely different to the rest of us, and it was therefore perhaps no surprise that your mother found him intriguing. Initially they became friends and eventually... eventually they were far more than that."

Adam felt a rush of cold down his spine accompanied by an unsettling sickly feeling in his stomach. Oddly now that the moment he had been waiting for had come, the chance to find out more about his past, he realised that he was afraid to hear any more. He felt like he was standing on the edge of a cliff, about to step off into the unknown. Once you started falling there was no stopping, no going back, just the ground waiting somewhere below and the vain hope that you would somehow land safely. He knew what Lucid was going to say before he spoke, although it didn't make it any less impossible. "As I think you may suspect, Hugo was your father."

CHAPTER 6

When he woke the following day, more than anything else Adam wanted to discuss the revelations of the night and his time in Reverie with someone. His head had been spinning ever since he had found the portrait and Lucid's halting explanation hadn't done anything to settle his mood. His connection to the pendant was clearer to him now, but the discoveries he'd made now raised other, bigger and far more complicated questions. He looked at himself in the mirror, leaning in towards his reflection more closely, trying to see if he could spot anything unusual. He thought back to the portrait and Hugo's strangely glowing eyes, prodding gently at the side of his own eyelids as he did so, but there was no glow from his own pupils, no sign of anything special anywhere in the reflection, not unless you counted slightly wonky ears and a couple of new spots.

Unfortunately for Adam there hadn't been anyone he could speak to, despite the fact that he felt like he would burst unless he could share his strange news with somebody. When he'd crossed the landing to use the bathroom in the morning Charlie's bedroom door had been closed and pausing for a moment, he hadn't been able to hear any sound coming from inside. He still wasn't downstairs by the time that Adam had finished his breakfast and when Charlie's mum joined him in the kitchen a few minutes later she admitted to him that, rather than feeling better, Charlie was feeling even worse than the previous day. Adam wasn't entirely surprised by this news, having struggled to get to sleep the night before, disturbed by the noise of footsteps going to and from the bathroom across the landing from his room, along with some more unpleasant sounds that he had tried to ignore.

"He's just feeling a bit run down and tired after a bit of a bad night," Mrs. Henson told him, in a voice which was meant to sound reassuring, although Adam couldn't really tell if she was trying to reassure him or herself.

"I hope he feels better soon," said Adam, as he pulled on his coat and grabbed his school bag. "I can let Miss Grudge know he won't be in today."

When Adam arrived at school and the morning register was called it was obvious that Charlie wasn't the only one off sick, with several other empty seats across the class. Halfway through the day things got even worse when Melanie Taylor suddenly fainted part way through their maths lesson and had to be sent home, her skin tinged with green as she was helped out the school gates by her anxious parents.

That afternoon Adam had planned to go to the Library again after school, needing to do some research for his latest school project. While it would now have to be without Charlie, he decided to go there anyway. He wanted to use the time, not only to do his school work but also to try and get his tumultuous thoughts a little straighter in his head. The alternative was to spend another evening making slightly awkward conversation with Mr. and Mrs. Henson, watching TV programmes about houses, gardens or most oddly, in Adam's opinion, watching programmes about people watching TV.

Adam had been sat in the Library for nearly an hour when he was disturbed, although not unpleasantly, by Nora's arrival. Initially she walked straight past the desk where he was seated, seeming not to have noticed him. However, he was pretty sure he saw her eyes dart across to him as she passed and there was what looked like a slight blush of embarrassment on her cheeks.

It was a few minutes later when she made her way back over to the desk and rather hesitantly took the seat opposite him. "Do you mind if I sit here?" she asked, nervous eyes catching his and then quickly looking down again. Adam smiled in what he hoped was a reassuring way. "Sure... I mean of course, no problem."

"I wanted to talk to you," she said. "I think that there are a few things that we need to talk about." Adam could feel his stomach tightening as she spoke. He had expected that this day would come, having been increasingly convinced over time that Nora remembered more of her time in Reverie than she had been letting on. But despite this, and even though he had played out this situation a dozen times in his head, he still felt completely unprepared, more nervous than when he had faced off against an army of Nightmares.

"What did you want to talk about?" he asked, not wanting to be the first one to mention Reverie and their shared experiences. Nora looked around quickly and seeming to be reassured by the emptiness of the Library, took a deep breath and leant in slightly towards Adam. "You remember when I was off school a little while ago?"

"Yes, of course," Adam replied, "we were all worried about you."

"I think that you know more about the time when I was um... ill than most people," Nora said, trying again to make eye contact with Adam as she spoke, but apparently finding it difficult, with her pupils darting off to one side within moments.

Adam stayed silent, waiting to see if Nora had anything further to say. "Look," she said, after the silence had stretched out just long enough to become uncomfortable, "either the next thing I say will make you think I am crazy, or it will be something that you understand, and will stop me thinking that I might be crazy myself." She stopped for a moment, gathering her courage and looked up again, this time managing to hold Adam's gaze. He could see something in her eyes that he recognised all too well. Something close to desperation, a need to be understood, to not be the only one who had experienced something unbelievable. These were all things which Adam had felt himself after his time in Reverie. As a result he immediately forgot his careful promise to himself that he wouldn't admit to knowing about the other world until she did.

"You're talking about when we met in the dream world," he said, the words spilling out before he could stop them. As soon as he said it he could see the reaction in Nora's face, her eyes widening in recognition and the corners of her mouth turning up in the very earliest stages of a relieved smile.

"It's true then," she breathed. "It's all real... I knew it."

"Look," said Adam, peering back over his shoulder as a chatting couple walked in, "maybe we should talk more about this... somewhere else, where we can talk properly."

As they walked down the street away from the Library Adam wondered where their conversation was going to take them next. It was a relief, in a way, to know that there was someone else he could talk to that really understood, that had also been to Reverie. He could talk about it to Charlie of course, and he had done that so often he now felt like Charlie knew the place nearly as well as he did, but it still wasn't the same as having actually been there. Pulling his attention back to the present he turned to Nora and was about to ask her more about her memories of her time in Reverie when he realised that she wasn't paying him any attention at all. Instead she was distracted by the sight of a small dog sat in the middle of the footpath, a couple of metres in front of them.

Adam didn't know too much about dogs but thought he recognised it as a Pomeranian. This one looked particularly fluffy and harmless and wasn't any taller than Adam's knee, but he still felt a strange moment of disquiet. There was something about the way that it was sat entirely still, seeming to be watching them both intently with its small dark eyes, which he found extremely unnerving. "Hello there," he heard Nora say in a friendly voice, crouching down to stroke the dogs head, then a moment later she suddenly recoiled, barreling back into Adam and nearly knocking him over.

"What on earth..." Adam began, wondering if the dog had tried to bite her, before he spotted what had made Nora react in the way she had. The Pomeranian was sat exactly where it had been before, and while it remained unmoving, Adam could see a dark, shadowy film in its eyes. As he stared at it the dog slowly stood up from its sitting position, raising it hackles aggressively and then took a step towards them, giving a louder, deeper and generally much scarier growl than the little dog should have been able to produce.

Nora was still staring in shock and didn't initially react when Adam grabbed hold of her hand and dragged her back away from the dog. "Come on!" he shouted at her, trying to snap her out of her daze. Slowly Nora seemed to regain her senses and looking down she shook her hand free of Adam's grip. Within a few moments Adam was struggling to keep pace with her as she sprinted down the street ahead of him, casting an occasional look back over her shoulder as she ran. Adam also risked a look back, the dog was about twenty metres behind them, its short legs whirling. Despite the obvious danger, Adam couldn't help but think how ridiculous the scene must appear, with the two of them running down the street as if their lives depended on it, being pursued by a tiny dog that wouldn't look out of place perched in a handbag.

As he ran Adam patted around his pockets, realising pretty quickly that he had forgotten to bring any of the bags of herbs from the dream world which he had used in the past to fend off Nightmares. Ever since he had saved Nora and defeated Isenbard he had presumed, it now seemed wrongly, that any danger he had faced was over and as a result he had stopped taking his previous careful precautions.

Digging deep and finding a bit more speed in his increasingly tired legs he managed to catch up with Nora and breathlessly pointed her in the direction of the park, which they could cut through to reach Charlie's house. While he didn't particularly want to lead the nightmare dog there, he had several of the bags of herbs in his room and couldn't think of anything else that would help. While the pendant around his neck had helped him escape a Nightmare in the Waking World once before, it wasn't something that he seemed fully able to control or trigger, so this seemed like the only option. Nora nodded, seeming to understand what he meant, and without slowing she cut across onto the footway that led through the middle of the park, her feet kicking up the gathered piles of autumn leaves as she ran. Following Nora up the path he took another quick look over his shoulder and saw the dog, still close behind. While it wasn't gaining on them it didn't seem to be dropping behind either, despite its tiny legs. It also didn't appear to be tiring, whereas Adam could feel the first burn of a stitch in his side and his lungs were definitely beginning to hurt. Nora was still a few paces ahead of him, rapidly approaching the large duck pond in the centre of the park, the footway skirting close to the nearest bank.

As he followed Adam felt his feet give way as he skidded on some loose gravel, his perspective suddenly and uncomfortably shifting, and with a painful bump he found himself looking at the bright blue sky between gaps in the canopy of the overhanging trees. Everything around him was slightly blurry, made hazy by his sudden fall and the resulting clash with the hard ground. Pushing himself up onto his elbows he shook his head in an attempt to clear the sudden cobwebs and as he did his hearing also began to return to normal. Unfortunately the first thing he heard was a deep, menacing growl and the first thing he saw, as his gaze moved back down from the blue sky above him, was a rapidly approaching, very tiny, fluffy but still (somehow) extremely evil looking dog.

Automatically Adam began scrabbling backwards, away from the approaching danger, but he was already aware that this wouldn't be nearly enough. By the time he got to his feet the dog would already be on him. He reached instinctively for the pendant around his neck, but his brain was still too fuzzy to focus and he felt no response from it. By now the Pomeranian was only a handful of metres away and without a pause he saw it launch itself through the air towards his face. Instinctively Adam went to curl up protectively, drawing his legs in towards his stomach. More by luck than anything else this meant that the first thing that the dog met was his feet rather than his face and for a moment Adam could feel its full weight resting on the soles of his shoes. Without stopping to think he rolled slightly further back and pushed out with his legs as hard as he could manage. While the dog was undoubtedly determined and oddly terrifying despite its size, the fact remained that it was also small and therefore weighed very little, as a result Adam managed to launch it quite some distance over his head. Moments later he heard a loud splash, followed by a very satisfying yelp.

Adam pushed himself over onto his stomach, turning to face the pond as he did so, and was greeted with the welcome sight of the Pomeranian, fluffy coat now waterlogged and bedraggled splashing through the water towards him. The side of the pond proved to be far too steep and slippery for the dog's short legs to manage. With a yowl of frustration it turned and started to make its way in a despondent doggy paddle towards the opposite, shallower bank.

Adam heaved himself onto his feet, and as quickly as he could, made his way around the pond to where Nora was now waiting by the gate to the park. "We... should... keep... moving," said Adam, catching his breath. "I don't want to be here when that thing gets out. Although I don't understand why a Nightmare would still be after us, I thought we had stopped Isenbard."

"I think there might be another reason why it's here," Nora admitted in between deep, gasping breaths, leaning forward with her hands on her knees. Adam looked across at her enquiringly, "and that is?" Nora slowly straightened back to a standing position, her breathing still heavy but less ragged than it had been. "I'll explain when we get back..." She paused at Adam's expression. "...I will, honestly."

It only took a few minutes to walk back across to Charlie's house. Mr. and Mrs. Henson were both sat in the living room, so Adam and Nora went straight up to his room, although Adam did shout a quick "Hi" to them both as he walked past the open door. As he made his way up the stairs to the landing he could see that the door to Charlie's bedroom was still closed and although he wanted to check on his friend, for the moment he pointed Nora through to his room and pulled the door shut behind them.

"So what was it you wanted to tell me?" Adam asked, sitting down on the beanbag in the corner of the room. But rather than explain what had just happened Nora seemed to be fascinated by Adam's room and was looking around at the bright decoration with a playful grin on her face, momentarily distracted from the drama of the earlier chase.

"Nice room," she said, taking in the candyfloss coloured wallpaper and horribly patterned curtains. "Not really what I expected, but it's nice that you have chosen a theme and stuck with it... good for you."

"Yeah, thanks," Adam replied sarcastically. "It took a really long time to find a Rabbit and Unicorn patterned bedspread that I was truly happy with, but I refused to give up until I found just the right one..." He paused, not sure that his sarcasm was getting through. "You do know that this was Charlie's sister's room don't you?" he asked a little more sheepishly. Nora's grin widened "Yes, but it's still fun to wind you up about it."

She sat down on the edge of the bed and sighed, the grin fading to be replaced by a far more serious expression. "Okay, I need to explain about earlier," she began reluctantly, not seeming to want to move on to more serious topics. "Like I said, I think that there is a particular reason why the Nightmares might be after me... and it's not just because of what happened before... although it is connected to that."

Adam didn't say anything for a moment, waiting for Nora to continue with her explanation, but she was obviously nervous and he could see that she was struggling to find a way to say what she wanted to. "I've seen a lot of very strange things lately..." he said, as reassuringly as he could "...and I have had to explain some really difficult things to Charlie... and to you, things that I never thought would make sense to anyone else. So don't worry, I'm sure there's nothing you could say that would surprise me that much."

"Thanks," Nora said, appearing to come to a decision within herself, "but I think it might be easier if I show you rather than try and explain," and she looked directly into Adam's eyes. For a second as their gaze locked a small part of his brain noticed the flecks of brown in the green surrounding her pupils, then something completely unexpected happened. A slick blackness flooded across her eyeballs, causing Adam to gasp in surprise. He unconsciously pushed himself as far back from Nora's face as he could, almost tipping himself backwards off the beanbag as a result. One hand went automatically to the pendant hanging around his neck, the other held out protectively in front of him.

"No... wait, please," Nora said. To Adam's surprise she was still speaking in her own voice, rather than the cold, emotionless tone he had come to associate with the Incubo, "it's not what you think....or at least not exactly what you think."

The blackness had left her eyes and she seemed, as far as Adam could tell, to still be herself. "What on earth was that?" Adam asked, aware that he was currently sprawled awkwardly half off the back of the beanbag and not looking very heroic at all. Taking a moment to reposition himself he looked back across at Nora to see if there was any further sign of the darkness crossing her eyes.

"Like I said," Nora continued once Adam had settled himself, "it's not what you think."

"What I think," replied Adam, as calmly as he could manage, "is that you have one of the Incubo hiding in there somewhere. I saw it in your eyes, or at least I am pretty sure I did."

At this Nora did something that caught Adam by complete surprise, she nodded slightly. "Yes, you're right....ever since I was taken to the dream world and was kept trapped in that horrible nightmare. One of the things you call an Incubo, one of the intelligent Nightmares was sent to keep a watch on me, guard me. I didn't know at the time that was what they were called, just that something was watching over me."

"You almost make it sound like it was looking after you, not keeping you prisoner," Adam said, still completely thrown by Nora's halting explanation.

"That's exactly it," Nora replied. "It was guarding me to begin with... but I was alone in that nightmare for weeks and..." She stopped for a moment, unpleasant memories bubbling to the surface. "I know it sounds unbelievable, but the Incubo started to talk to me. Over time it felt... sorry for me, kept me company. If it hadn't been there I don't know how I would have managed, left alone for all that time."

Adam stared at Nora dumbfounded. "Just because it spoke to you doesn't make it good or nice," he said. "I mean they are really not nice at all...they do terrible things."

"Not this one," replied Nora, more firmly. "Mittens isn't like the others; she's nice. When I escaped with you she stayed with me and... she doesn't really want to go back into the dream world." She rubbed her fingers unconsciously across the strands of the friendship bracelet wrapped around the wrist of her right arm. One that Adam was pretty sure she hadn't been wearing a moment before.

Adam was still struggling to take in everything that Nora was saying, so it took a moment for her last comment to sink in. "Mittens?" he asked in disbelief. "You called it Mittens."

"She..." muttered Nora, a little defensively, "....Mittens isn't an 'it', Mittens is a 'she'."

"Unbelievable," Adam muttered, half to himself. "Absolutely unbelievable. I spend all my time running from Nightmares and you've been carrying one around with you," he looked pointedly at her new friendship bracelet "...and now it has a name." Although he was still reeling from the shock he was feeling he couldn't help himself. "...also why on earth call it Mittens?" he added, horribly fascinated despite himself.

For a moment Nora had the good grace to look slightly embarrassed. "Mittens was my cat when I was little. When I was trapped for so long in that horrible dream I pretended that she was still there to keep me company." She scowled across at Adam, daring him to laugh at her. "You don't know what it was like, it was awful trapped in there for so long. So when the Incubo started talking to me I called her Mittens… it made me feel better."

"Whatever," Adam muttered, "just seemed like a strangely cuddly choice of name for a Nightmare creature."

Nora grabbed his hand and looked straight into Adam's eyes for a moment, the slick blackness spilling back across her eyes. "Please believe me," she said, her voice oddly layered as if two different sets of vocal chords were now forming the words at the same time. "I know it's not easy to believe but Nora is telling the truth. I don't mean you or her any harm, I just…. I don't want to go back." Adam tried to pull his hand away, but Nora's grip was surprisingly strong as she continued. "We scare people, I know that, it's what we were made to do… and I admit I enjoy it. But recently things have been different in Reverie. We have been made to do far worse things, to cross into this world, to operate outside of the rules of the Great Dream. Not all of us agree with the changes, not all of us want to do the things we are told."

Adam didn't know how to react. Everything he had seen, everything he had experienced had taught him to be afraid of the Incubo. Lucid and Grimble had never expressed anything but fear and loathing for them and yet… he had felt none of the signs that had generally warned him of danger from the Nightmares when he had been with Nora, nor did he feel them now. There was no chill up his spine, no warning glow from his pendant. Nora released his hand, the darkness receding from her eyes, running back down her arm and re-forming around her wrist as the friendship bracelet appeared there once again. As it did the temporary intensity drained from her face, replaced instead with a look of nervous hope. "So," she said, "what do you think?"

"Is that just you talking again?" Adam asked. "The Incubo… Mittens has gone I mean."

Nora nodded. "It's hard to explain but yes, most of the time she stays out of the way, tries her best to give me some privacy. She doesn't come out unless I want her too." She paused for a moment running her fingers across the bracelet again as she spoke. "Umm... while she is gone, you should probably know that I told her that Mittens was the name for a great and terribly bloodthirsty warrior in our world. I think she is quite an important Nightmare in Reverie and might be offended if she realised that I had named her after a kitten. So please keep that to yourself okay?"

"Fine... although this might take a bit of getting used to," said Adam, still unsure how much he could trust Nora and whatever she was now carrying around with her. "But let's say I believe you, what do you intend to do. I mean... it seems like the Nightmares are going to keep coming for you and we won't always be lucky like we were this time."

Nora nodded, scrunching the end of her sleeves with nervous fingers as she spoke. "I know, I was hoping you might be able to help. You seemed to know how to deal with the Nightmares."

"Honestly it's mainly been either luck or help from other people," replied Adam as honestly as he could, ignoring a treacherous, sneaking desire to try and impress her. "But I can at least give you some of these," he added, leaning around and scrabbling in one of his drawers for some of the bags of herbs. "If you burn one of these bags the smoke seems to get rid of the Nightmares... at least for a while." Then he stopped and thought for a moment. "I would make sure you are well clear of the smoke yourself though, otherwise you could end up getting rid of Mittens without meaning to."

Nora pocketed the bags carefully and nodded again. "Thank you. I'll be careful, but in the meantime perhaps you could see if there is anything else you could do to help, anything you could find in the dream world?" She managed to re-find her smile, although it was a bit weak. "I feel sorry for Mittens and I want to help her, but I don't really want to carry her around forever..." Then she paused before adding a quick "...no offence."

For a moment her eyes swam with darkness once again. "None taken," she said in her oddly layered voice and smiled broadly at Adam.

CHAPTER 7

That night when Adam entered Reverie his mind still hadn't settled. The last week had been full of too many incredible revelations for him to properly deal with them all. First the earth-shattering discovery about his mother and Hugo, a dream being who could be his father. Then there was the news about Nora and the rather disturbing 'guest' she was carrying around. The way things were going he was pretty convinced that it was only a matter of time before Miss Grudge revealed herself to be the secret president of the world.

On the plus side, even with the tumult in his mind, he was still able to pinpoint the spot where Lucid was waiting for him. For the last couple of weeks he had been experimenting with attempts to enter Reverie in locations other than the clearing where he had first arrived with increasing success. After the first few tries he had realised he could find his way to places he had visited before, so long as he could picture it fully in his mind. He had also found that, as he entered the dream world, there was a brief moment when he could almost feel the flow of dreams and thoughts flying through the air around him. Tonight he had focused on finding Lucid, despite his distracted state, so it was with some satisfaction that he awoke a matter of metres from the spot where Lucid was sat patiently waiting in the gardens of the old mansion.

Despite his earlier discussion with Nora, Adam made a snap decision not to mention Mittens for the moment, as he wasn't at all sure how Lucid and Grimble would react. Instead he launched straight into a more neutral topic of conversation. "Any more news on the problems in Moonshine?"

"Not exactly, no," replied Lucid. "But I have arranged for us to visit Bombast at the Library, I believe that he may be able to help." He got to his feet and pointed Adam towards the door leading back through the mansion. "After that…" he continued "…we will travel by barge to Moonshine and see what is going on for ourselves…should be an interesting few days one way or another."

* * *

Bombast was sat behind his desk in the office of the Great Library when Lucid and Adam dropped in for their visit. "My friends, welcome," he boomed enthusiastically, rising strenuously to his feet and leaning forward with his hands resting on the desk as he did so, which creaked rather ominously. Smiling broadly he made his way around to them and grabbed Lucid by the shoulders, loudly planting a kiss on each cheek. "Good to see you again, it has been too long… and you have brought the young hero of Reverie with you again, I am privileged," he added, favouring Adam with a friendly wink. Muttering something about, "not being a hero and just doing what anyone would have done," in embarrassment, Adam still felt his chest swell, just a little, with pride at the reference.

As with their previous visit it seemed that they would be unable to simply have a conversation with Bombast without first being hugely fussed over. Holding up a finger to them to pause their conversation for a moment, (despite the fact that he was the one doing most of the talking), Bombast pulled down a small tube hanging from the side of wall close to his desk and used it to ask an unseen assistant, somewhere at the other end of the tube, to bring refreshments. "Sit, sit, please make yourselves comfortable," Bombast said, directing them to the comfy and deeply upholstered seats.

As he made his way over Adam spotted what looked like a new addition to the paintings that graced the office's opulent walls, taking pride of place in a particularly extravagant golden frame. It had been hung directly between the portrait showing Bombast as a knight slaying a dragon and another showing him as an explorer planting a flag on top of a snowy peaked mountain. This new painting showed an intrepid looking ship's captain stood brave and resolute on the deck of a boat caught in the centre of a tempestuous storm. It was no surprise to Adam that the captain once again bore a remarkable resemblance to Bombast, making him look even more like a giant pantomime pirate than normal.

"Aha… admiring the art once again," Bombast enthused, pointing to the new portrait. "I felt it was high time to celebrate my time on the Dwam. A most interesting time in my career that I must share with you one day."

"The Dwam?" Adam asked, intrigued despite himself and ignoring Lucid's surreptitious hand motions to not encourage Bombast any further, "is that the name of a ship?"

"No, no…" Bombast chuckled, warming to his favourite topic of conversation, namely himself. "The Dwam is the great sea of Dreams at the edge of our world. When I was a younger man I decided to see what was on the other side, fancying myself as a great explorer."

"But unfortunately that will have to be a tale for another day," Lucid broke in, politely but firmly. "I am afraid that we have other business that we need to discuss with you."

Deflating slightly Bombast nodded in reluctant acceptance. "Very well, another day then." Disappointment was obvious in his voice as he sat back down behind his desk, twiddling one of the pointed ends of his oiled beard absentmindedly. "So what is the business you speak of?"

"We leave shortly for Moonshine. The Queen has asked that we travel there to investigate some unusual goings on." Noting the rise in Bombast's eyebrows and the amused twinkle re-igniting within his eyes, Lucid quickly continued his explanation. "I am aware of Moonshine's reputation, Grimble will hardly let me forget, but I am told that this is something unusual even by Moonshine's standards, something particularly... troubling."

"So what can I do to help?" Bombast leant forward, his charcoal eyes switching between Adam and Lucid. "It has been a while but I suppose I could be convinced to break my old adventuring trousers back out of storage to help you youngsters out." He flexed his considerable shoulders as he spoke. "Hmmm, yes... might do me good to set the world to rights once again."

Turning to one side Adam could see Lucid sat next to him open-mouthed, his expression slipping slowly from mild amusement to one of scarcely contained horror. "No, no... I mean there is no need for that Bombast," Lucid said, trying his best to keep rising panic from his voice. "While I am sure you would be a great help, it's actually your advice that we came for."

Before he could go any further they were disturbed by one of the Library staff politely knocking on the office door before carefully backing into the room pulling a trolley carrying a variety of expensive looking snacks. There was also a large pot of tea and a set of matching, very delicate looking, china cups and saucers.

"Oh good..." Bombast rubbed his hands together at the sight, "perfect timing, talk of adventure always makes me peckish."

In between bites of intoxicatingly sweet soft pastries that reminded Adam of small, more intensely flavoured donuts, Lucid went back to the reason for their visit. "We know that Chimera are operating in Moonshine and the Queen suspects that they are doing something... untoward."

"Ah, and so you thought of me," said Bombast, his face becoming more serious.

"Sorry to bring you into this," Lucid told him, pausing eating for a moment and wiping a few stray crumbs from his chin, "but you know as much about Chimera as pretty much anyone I can think of."

Bombast sighed and leant back heavily in his chair, all signs of his previous good humour gone. "Chimera are a disease as far as I am concerned, meddling with things that shouldn't be meddled with, squeezing at the edges of the Great Dream just to milk out a little bit more profit." He banged the desk with his closed fist with surprising ferocity. "I told him not to get involved with them, but the idiot wouldn't listen." Catching Adam's eye, Bombast stopped for a moment to explain himself. "I speak of my brother, he works for the company and has done very well for himself. I suspect this is the reason Lucid has come for my advice."

Lucid nodded. "If anyone knows what Chimera are doing over in Moonshine then I imagine your brother might?"

"More than you would imagine," Bombast replied with a grimace. "I believe that he is most probably there now. He came to see me a couple of months ago, puffed up with his own importance, full of excitement about a new project he would be working on." Lucid leant forward at this point, obviously keen to hear more. "Is there anything you can tell us, anything you can think of that might help?"

"Nothing in particular," Bombast admitted. "He didn't share any details with me, just told me it was top secret and very exciting. The best I can do is to arrange for you to meet with him when you arrive in Moonshine. Chimera have almost paranoid levels of security, without an arranged introduction it is unlikely you would ever get past the front door."

"That would be appreciated Bombast, thank-you," said Lucid as he levered himself up from his seat, gesturing to Adam to do the same. "We don't really know what we are getting involved in, so anything that you could do would help us. But for now I am afraid that Adam and I will need to get underway."

As they opened the door to the office, heading back out into the main Library, Bombast called out one last time to them both, still sat at the desk, looking for the first time smaller and more human than the surrounding heroic paintings. "My brother... he is not a bad man, just a little weak and pompous, if he is mixed up in something bad then I doubt he knows it... please treat him as kindly as you can."

* * *

As he walked down the street that led from the Great Square which housed the Library to the Docks, where the Dreamskipper was waiting to ferry them across the Weave to their destination, Adam spotted a small figure walking towards them. From a distance it appeared to be a Sleepwalker. The boy was oblivious to his surroundings and walked in a straight line down the street, residents of the city stepping to one side to let him pass. As they did so several of them turned to stare more closely and Adam could hear them muttering to each other in surprise. As the boy approached it became clear what it was about him that was drawing their attention. Rather than the slow and measured pace of the Sleepwalkers that Adam had previously seen crossing the city, the boy's movement was faster and slightly erratic. As he drew close to Adam he could see that the boy's face looked flushed and feverish, a thin sheen of sweat on his skin. The only real similarity he had with the Sleepwalkers was a seeming ignorance of his surroundings, despite his wide and staring eyes. "What's up with him?" Adam asked, but Lucid could only shrug, looking as confused as Adam. "It's not something I have seen before," he admitted. "I can ask Grimble when we see him, he may have seen something like it before... but it is worrying." His brow creased, "very worrying indeed."

CHAPTER 8

By the middle of the afternoon Adam and the others were well on their way to Moonshine. Grimble had been waiting for them morosely at the docks when they arrived. He was already on board Lucid's barge, the Dreamskipper, glumly resigned to the fact that, not only was he going to have to travel to Moonshine, but he would have to do so by boat. After boarding they had briefly discussed the strange Sleepwalker, but their description of the boy hadn't meant anything to Grimble either and they had ended the conversation no wiser.

After this initial discussion the rest of their journey on the Dreamskipper had been largely uneventful. Adam had used this opportunity to rest his head for a while, spending most of his time lounging on the deck and letting his mind wander. It was nearing the evening when Lucid finally disturbed his rest. "Just ahead of us is Whimsy," Lucid informed him, as they made their way around a long, meandering bend in the Weave. "It is the last village before we head into the more… unusual parts of Reverie, so I would suggest that we moor up there for the night before continuing our journey tomorrow."

"Fine," Grimble muttered, not looking happy with the suggestion, before limping off to the other end of the barge and leaning heavily on the railings, staring out into the distance.

"What's up with Grimble?" Adam asked Lucid quietly. "He seems pretty unhappy about something." He paused for a moment, "…I mean more unhappy than normal."

"Whimsy holds memories for him, bad ones," Lucid replied. "You remember we spoke of the previous Horror that Grimble and his companions faced?"

Adam nodded "When Isenbard betrayed them?"

"Exactly, that took place here. So as you can imagine, even though it was some time ago, visiting here is still difficult for him."

Adam looked back across at Grimble, still staring out into the distance, although it was hard to tell if he was looking out at the horizon or at something much further away, remembering the past.

When Adam got his first glimpse of Whimsy it was very much as he had imagined from the name, a small village nestled close to the banks of the Weave, picture book pretty with clusters of stone cottages, thatched roofs and winding paved lanes. As they drew up to the small dock several children scampered up to the edge of the village and stared in open-mouthed fascination at them. They continued giggling amongst themselves, pointing as Lucid stepped across the small gap from the deck of the Dreamskipper onto the planks of the jetty and tied up the barge. Then he beckoned across to Adam and Grimble to follow him and started to wander up the rough stone path leading to the centre of the village. Adam made his way quickly after him, although Grimble followed more hesitantly, lagging some way behind. Unusually for him, he also kept the hood of his plain robe raised, casting most of his face into shadow.

As he walked Adam glanced from side to side at the low stone cottages that made up most of the village, roughly finished stone blocks expertly slotted into place leaving almost no gaps between them, the few little remaining crevices filled with a grassy moss. Out of several of these gaps there were also small clusters of flowers growing, making every wall, no matter how plain, come alive with life and colour. The group of children was still following them, although at a distance, too far away for Adam to make out the content of their excited, high pitched chattering as he sped up, trying to catch up with Lucid.

As he rounded the next corner he saw that Lucid had stopped to wait for them, having reached the small open clearing in the centre of the village. He was talking easily with a tall, powerfully built and rather intimidating looking man, stopping to turn and wave to Adam as he drew closer. "Adam," Lucid greeted him, "this is Steffen, the village chief. He was apparently told to expect our arrival and has lodgings prepared for us in one of the cottages."

"You are very welcome," Steffen told him with a smile, the cheerful expression a pleasant surprise on his craggy, grey-bearded face. Adam could see signs of scarring across his face, leaving his friendly smile slightly uneven, making Adam think of the similar looking marks that Grimble had suffered. "Anyone who is willing to help us with the troubles in Moonshine is worthy of our hospitality."

"Thanks, I really appreciate it," Adam replied, grateful for the warm welcome and the chance to fall asleep, and to travel back to his own world, somewhere comfortable for a change.

Steffen directed them to one of the cottages that faced out onto the small village green before politely excusing himself, leaving to shoo away a number of the children that had continued to follow them. He was only partly successful, with the bolder and more inquisitive youngsters quickly circling around to the back of the cottage instead, where they continued to stare and gossip.

It was only when Adam wondered why Grimble wasn't shouting some sort of grumpy reprimand at the children that he realised that their companion was no longer behind them. "Do you know where Grimble's gone?" he asked. Lucid gestured over towards the far edge of the village. "I suspect he will be off revisiting his memories. While he may be looking for some time alone, if you want to truly understand what happened here before then perhaps you could go and find him?" Adam nodded and left Lucid to settle into their new lodgings, walking in the general direction Lucid had indicated and wondering what he would find.

As he travelled further away from the central village green Adam could almost physically feel the change in atmosphere. The air was thicker and heavier, with the sense of fresh, natural goodness that had spilled out from the rest of the village, so comfortably nestled into the surrounding landscape, replaced slowly by a far sadder and emptier sensation that seemed to seep up from the ground and increasingly surrounded him as he walked. The low, solid looking cottages he passed as he reached the outskirts were all empty, with the mossy growths that coloured the sides of the occupied homes grown wilder, slowly eating their way across the walls. As he reached the very edge of the village the state of the houses became even worse. Rather than being purely overgrown or rundown, the walls of these were stained black, the stone heavily corroded. The windows and doors that had once been fitted into the stone walls were all long gone, the glass shattered and the wooden frames rotted away. The front of these homes were reduced to open, staring husks that sent a chill down Adam's spine. It was there, on the very edge of the village, that he found Grimble, squatting down with his hand pressed against the wall of one of the abandoned cottages.

Although he didn't turn around it seemed that Grimble had heard him approaching, rising slowly from his kneeling position. "I didn't think I would ever come here a second time," he said, still not turning to face Adam. His voice was quieter than normal, but heavy with remembered pain. "I didn't want to ever see this place again, but here we are. It seems that whatever I do, fate is determined to not let me forget. First Isenbard returns and then we have to stop here on our way to Moonshine."

"Is that why... why you hated the thought of going to Moonshine so much?" Adam asked him. Grimble shrugged, a relaxed motion that didn't really seem to match the tightness in his voice. "Who knows... maybe, I never liked Moonshine much anyway. The place is a mess... it's amazing that it continues to function at all. But I would have to admit that the place also holds particularly bad memories."

Although Adam was keen to know more, he didn't want to pry further into something so obviously private and painful, so instead he waited quietly and was rewarded when Grimble continued to talk, finally turning to face him. "It was many years ago that I was here last, back when your mother was part of the Five. Back when Isenbard led us. A more optimistic time, we were all younger... we felt we could do anything." Ears pricking up at another mention of his mother, Adam stayed silent, hoping that Grimble would share more. "We had been called out to deal with the appearance of a Horror, a relatively small one. It should have been easy."

A suspicion had been growing in Adam's mind while Grimble had been speaking, so he asked, as gently as he could, "Was it Deliria who called you out here?"

"It was," Grimble admitted with a sigh. "She said that the Horror was headed towards Moonshine and that we could intercept it here. We got here in plenty of time, prepared ourselves working with the villagers to divert some of the Weave so we could block the progress of the Horror, as we and our predecessors had successfully done on several occasions before."

As he spoke Grimble slowly limped across from the scorched building to a spot a few metres outside of the village boundary where a deep and darkly stained trench remained, cut into the landscape. A few plants had made a spirited attempt to grow down the sides, but they looked sickly and discoloured, fighting a losing battle against the lingering malignance left by the Horror. "It was here," he said, hardly seeming to be speaking to Adam now, lost in memories. "It was here that we expected to stop it... but Isenbard had left a small gap in the trench, a flaw in our defence that let the Horror through. Suddenly all our planning meant nothing and it was upon us, moving into the village."

Adam looked around at the scorched, empty cottages and tried to imagine them as lively, happy occupied homes, bursting with activity like the others in the centre of Whimsy. "We eventually managed to stop the Horror, even after Isenbard's betrayal," Grimble continued, "but we lost one of ours, Lucid's predecessor, Spindle... and Hugo was badly injured, buying the rest of us the time necessary to reform our defence."

Thinking back to the slim, dark-haired man in the portrait Adam couldn't stop himself from asking, "So what happened to Hugo?" Grimble shrugged uncomfortably. "No one fully knows. He was wounded and seemed unlikely to pull through, despite his unnatural strength. Your mother was inconsolable, although we tried our best to comfort her." His expression darkened for a moment. "She was determined that he could be saved, regardless of the cost or consequence. Shortly after the attack she disappeared along with Hugo and until very recently, that was the last we saw of either of them. Then just before the most recent Horror she got back in touch with Lucid and... you know the rest."

Adam nodded, a thought had begun to germinate in the back of his mind as Grimble had told his story. The portrait of his mother and Hugo swimming its way back across his brain. In particular the image of the pendant hanging around her neck kept pushing itself to the forefront of his attention. He remembered the voice that had warned him of the Nightmares, a voice that had seemed to come from within the pendant. A voice that he hadn't known and yet had seemed oddly familiar to him all the same. His hand crept unconsciously back to the spot where the pendant hung loosely under his t-shirt and for a moment he was sure he felt a pulse of warmth from it.

For the moment however Adam's suspicion remained just that, a vague theory that he couldn't prove... and which he wasn't quite ready to share. Fortunately Grimble was still caught up in his own memories and hadn't seemed to notice Adam's reaction to his story. Instead Grimble straightened up and lowered his hood revealing his heavily scarred face once again, an unavoidable daily reminder of his previous clash with the Horror. "Come on," said Grimble gruffly. "I think that's enough memories for one day. Let's get back to the village, we need to leave early tomorrow if we are going to reach Moonshine on time."

Looking again at Grimble's scars Adam thought back to the similar injuries he had seen on Steffen, the Village Chief's face.

"Was Steffen there at the time of the last Horror?" he asked, try-ing not to stare at the scars as he did. Grimble's mouth twisted into an ironic smile at his question. "Heh... you've seen him then. Yes he was there. He was much younger at the time and quite the lady's man, but it turned out that he was also surpris-ingly brave. He stuck with us even when things went bad and now he and I can compete for who has the prettiest face." He twisted his features into a scowling grimace, about as close to a smile as Adam had seen on his face for a while.

The rest of the walk back to the centre of the village passed mainly in silence, both Adam and Grimble having too much on their minds to spend further time talking. Within a few minutes they had drawn close to the central green and as they did, Adam saw a cluster of the villagers stood slightly nervously to one side. To start with Adam wondered if their nerves were caused by his arrival, or that of his companions, but then he noticed a young girl walking jerkily across the square. Similar to the odd figure he had seen on his way to the Dreamskipper back in Nocturne, initially the girl looked like a Sleepwalker, seem-ingly unaware of her surroundings. "Look," he said to Grimble, indicating the girl. "She's like the boy Lucid and I saw, the one we told you about."

Grimble grunted in acknowledgment and they walked nearer to the girl to get a better look. As they drew closer Adam could see a thin sheen of sweat on her face and an unhealthy looking greenish tinge to her skin. "Odd," muttered Grimble, "I have never seen this before."

Amongst the cluster of villagers Adam spotted Steffen, the village chief, who walked briskly across to them, raising his hand in greeting. "You saw the Girl?" Steffen asked, his bushy, grey eyebrows raised in question. Grimble nodded in confirm-ation. "Recently we have seen several of these odd dreamers," Steffen continued, "and we have heard talk of many more being spotted around Moonshine." His expression grew darker. "The timing of their appearance matches the arrival of Chimera... and the opening of their new factory. It may be a coincidence of course, but it seemed worth investigating further. We have made representations to them, but they deny any link between their work and these strange Sleepwalkers... strenuously."

"We will be meeting with someone at Chimera tomorrow," Grimble told him, "hopefully we will find out more then."

"You best be careful how you deal with them," Steffen said with a dark look. "Chimera are extremely secretive about what they are doing and are very... sensitive to any sort of criticism."

"Thanks for the advice," Grimble replied, on this occasion Adam getting the impression that he genuinely meant it, then he wished Steffen goodnight before heading quickly back to the cottage with Adam. Lucid was sat waiting in the main room, a plate of bread and cheese laid out for each of them, along with an oddly, although pleasantly, flavoured herbal drink. "We saw another one of the strange Sleepwalkers..." Adam told him in between mouthfuls, "...and the village chief said that they have seen several of them across Moonshine, all since Chimera started working in the area."

Lucid nodded as Adam spoke, concern clear on his expressive face. "We will see what tomorrow brings," he said. "But I am beginning to see now why Deliria was worried and why she felt it necessary to ask for our help."

CHAPTER 9

The following day Adam couldn't concentrate, time passing painfully slowly as he waited for night to come and the chance to re-join Lucid and Grimble. For the first time he felt like he was getting close to finding out the truth about his parents and his past, so spending his day doing regular things like eating breakfast or sitting in lessons was almost impossible to bear. It didn't help that Charlie was still stuck in bed, no better than he had been the previous two days. Adam could tell that, despite Mrs. Henson's forced cheerfulness as they shared breakfast in the morning, she was starting to get genuinely worried about him. It was not a big surprise when he overheard her on the phone late that afternoon, just as he returned home from school, trying to book an appointment at the Doctors.

"What do you mean, nothing this week?" concern and scarcely contained frustration mixed uncomfortably in her voice. "He's really ill. He hasn't eaten anything for the last two days and... I see, okay I will have to try out of hours at the Hospital then." She put the telephone handset down heavily and turned to her husband. "They haven't got anything this week at all," she sighed in exasperation. "Apparently this sickness bug is almost an epidemic now and they are fully booked by other parents and children who are all showing the same symptoms as Charlie." Mr. Henson smiled back as reassuringly as he could at his wife, but even from across the room Adam could see he was worried too. "We will sort it out," he said, "if Charlie isn't any better by tomorrow then I'll take him down to the out of hours drop-in."

Although he hadn't really known what to say to either of

them, Adam was increasingly convinced in his own mind that there was more to Charlie's illness than a normal bug or fever. The sudden sickness that had affected Charlie and quite a few others at the school had arrived too close to the oddness now taking place in Reverie for it all to be a coincidence. More than that, he was also pretty sure that if he looked around long enough in the dream world he would eventually recognise one of the feverish Sleepwalkers as an absent classmate or friend. "Is it okay if I pop into his room for a few minutes to see how Charlie is feeling before I go to bed?" Adam asked them as he left the living room later that evening. "Of course," said Mrs. Henson, "but don't keep him talking too long."

When Adam went into Charlie's room he had to squint slightly as his eyes slowly adjusted to the darkness. There was also an unpleasant smell of lingering sickness and sweat that he tried to ignore as he made his way across to the bed. Charlie was half sat up, shoulders and neck resting on a couple of folded pillows. He smiled weakly as Adam approached, his eyes red and bloodshot. "Hello mate," he said, voice raspy. "Alright there," Adam replied a little guiltily. "Sorry I haven't checked on you for a bit. Your Mum said you weren't to be disturbed... that you were too ill."

"It's fine," Charlie reassured him, then paused for a moment to have a painful sounding coughing fit. "Besides, she's right... I am too ill."

Adam looked at his best friend and tried to keep the concern he felt out of his voice. "You said before that you started to feel ill straight after a strange dream?" Charlie's brow creased for a moment at Adam's line of questioning and then he nodded. "That's right. I felt fine when I went to bed, had a really odd dream and then when I woke up I felt like this." He broke out into another coughing fit, which only calmed after Adam passed him a glass of water. "Ugh... I hate this," Charlie croaked. "I feel rotten and really, really tired, but I swear every time I manage to get some sleep it just gets worse rather than better."

"I think that's something to do with this illness," Adam said.

"I might be completely wrong about this, but there is some really strange stuff going on in Reverie and I think it might have something to do with whatever is making people sick here."

Charlie raised his eyebrows slightly in disbelief. "Might just be the flu you know, not everything always has to have a weird, supernatural reason." He coughed again, covering his mouth with his hand and wincing as the violence of the cough shook his body in a series of painful-looking spasms. "Still, I suppose it can't do any harm to check," he managed to splutter between coughs.

"Can you remember anything about your dream?" Adam asked him. "Just in case there really is some sort of link. It could really help."

Charlie closed his eyes, his brow furrowed in concentration. "I can't remember all the details," he admitted wearily, "but if you really think it would be helpful... I'll try my best." He made an effort to push himself upright in the bed, although he slumped back against the stacked cushions with a groan after a moment. "I remember everything being strange. More strange than normal for a dream I mean. I remember feeling really hungry and thirsty and then stopping somewhere, I can't remember where, to have a drink. Then it got really odd, the world was spinning around me, the colours of everything around me were suddenly far too bright and in the background there was this insane music playing over and over... and there was a voice speaking behind it all, but I couldn't really hear what it was saying."

As he spoke Adam could see the effort that the recollection was taking. Charlie's face was running with sweat and his cheeks were flushed with fever. "I remember one other thing," he said. "It's just come back to me. When I was looking around, just before it got really weird, there was a sign I walked past, like one of the signs in old American movies at the entrance to a town." Adam nodded, remembering any number of happy nights spent watching old films and munching popcorn with his friend. "I remember now," said Charlie. "I remember what the sign had on it, it said 'Welcome to Moonshine'."

When Adam returned to Reverie that night, Charlie's most recent words were still going around in his head. Despite this, he managed once again to concentrate just about enough to pinpoint Lucid's location and as a result he woke, rather uncomfortably, on the deck of the Dreamskipper. It seemed he had rejoined his companions just in time, as they were about to reach their destination. Both Lucid and Grimble were more tense than usual when he tried speaking to them, so he decided to sit quietly instead.

He could feel Moonshine before he saw it. An odd prickly feeling across his skin, the sensation very similar to goosebumps. Then as they cleared the corner of the last bend in the Weave a most unusual sight opened up to them. There, sat sprawled along the banks was the oddest mass of mismatched, gaudy and in many cases downright ugly buildings that Adam had ever seen. Right in the centre of the city was a brightly coloured fairy-tale palace, with pointed towers at every corner, each one topped with a flag fluttering wildly in the breeze. The rest of the city was clustered in slightly haphazard concentric circles around the palace, the densest and most solidly constructed buildings closest to its walls. Further from the palace the buildings were far more poorly built, some on the very outskirts appearing to be little more than a few planks and sheets of canvas randomly thrown together. Above the city the air was hazy, filled with a light pink smog, swirling in the morning breeze.

"Welcome to Moonshine," said Lucid with a slightly sarcastic flourish.

"It looks... a bit unusual," Adam replied, not really sure what to make of his first impression of the place.

"Bah!" Grimble broke in with a scowl. "It doesn't get any better, believe me."

"But our first stop isn't the main port," Lucid continued. "We need to head straight to the Chimera building. Bombast has arranged a meeting with his brother for us and he is expecting us..." he stopped to check his watch "...any time now."

Looking along the far bank, the Chimera offices were easy enough to identify, totally out of place compared to their more bohemian and colourful surroundings. The main building was a large, functional looking rectangular block sat right on the banks of the Weave, with the only attempt at architecture being two tall, dark glazed windows running vertically across several floors. From a distance these looked like a pair of huge eyes staring dolefully out from the front of the building. Off to one side of this there was a smaller, although still huge, domed building, also fronting the Weave.

The building was also apparently sufficiently busy to require its own private dock. This meant that Lucid was able to steer the Dreamskipper into a berth close to the offices, rather than docking in the city and having to make the remainder of their journey on foot. Whatever other misgivings they had about Chimera, it was clear that they were very well organised and efficient. Within minutes of docking they had safely tethered their barge, Lucid had signed all the necessary paperwork with the dock-master, and they were well on their way to the main building.

Above the main doors hung a large sign with an image on it which Adam identified once again as a Chimera, the dream creature after which he assumed the company had been named. Walking up to the main entrance, located centrally between the two large eye-like windows, Adam couldn't help but feel that he was entering the mouth of a huge beast. Mentally shaking himself free of such silly thoughts he crossed the threshold, following Lucid and Grimble up to the main reception desk where several members of staff were sat behind a surprisingly secure looking set of brass railings.

"Welcome to the offices of the Chimera and Reverie Holding Company," said the tall and rather superior looking man sat at the centre of the desk, his slow drawl making him sound incredibly bored despite his apparent efficiency. "How may I assist you?"

"We are here to see Mr. Rapscallion," Grimble told him. "He should be expecting us."

The tall man nodded and smiled thinly before checking a sheet of paper off to one side. "Ah yes," he tapped his finger part way down the sheet. "If you three...'gentlemen' would please follow me to Mr. Rapscallion's offices," he informed them, before leaving the reception desk through a solid looking gate, which snapped firmly closed again behind him. Adam wasn't particularly keen on the half-hearted way the word 'gentlemen' had been used, and it was clear from a number of the more colourful gestures Grimble was now making behind the man's back as they began the walk across the office that he obviously felt the same.

The building was a hive of activity, with groups of important looking people constantly crisscrossing the wide, open foyer area. Some were carrying handfuls of paper, while others were simply walking purposefully, but they all looked extremely busy. Several wore long white jackets that reminded Adam of the lab coats from science lessons in school, others were in smart-looking suits and a third group were wearing dark overalls with shiny badges featuring the Chimera symbol. Adam presumed this third group were some sort of security, although he was a bit surprised at just how many security staff there seemed to be, outnumbering both the scientists and the office workers.

After a brisk walk down the nearest corridor, following the tall receptionist like a group of ducklings trailing after a particularly snooty mother duck, Adam and the others arrived at a set of double doors set into the nearest wall. The receptionist knocked once at the doors before opening the left hand one of the pair and gesturing for them to enter.

The room they entered was positioned to provide a view of the Weave through one of the large windows Adam has spotted on the approach to the building. He presumed that offices with a view like that were highly sought after, which meant that Bombast's brother must be pretty important.

In the centre of the far wall, located to make the most of this view, was a wide dark wooden desk and behind that sat an imposing figure, tall and substantially built. Adam could immediately see the family resemblance to Bombast, although rather than the theatrical dress that Bombast tended to favour, the man behind the desk was in a sharply tailored but conservative suit, the dark material of the jacket offset against an expanse of crisp white shirt. The only allowance for colour was a pair of bright red elasticated braces which seemed to be just about winning an ongoing battle to hold the man's trousers in place.

Slowly heaving himself to his feet the man leant forward across the desk and extended a large hand in greeting as they approached, shaking first Lucid's, then Grimble's and finally Adam's hand with a surprisingly gentle grip. "Clement Earp Rapscallion the third, pleased to meet you." He paused for a moment and winced. "You must excuse the name, it has always been a source of slight embarrassment, especially in the business world, but it's an old family name, you know how these things are." Adam nodded, although he wasn't sure how sincere either the wince or the explanation were, both seeming rather too well rehearsed. He was also a little distracted by the thought that there must have already been a Clement Earp Rapscallion the first and second. "Bombast told me that you had something you wanted to discuss," Clement continued. "I will obviously do my best to help friends of my dear older brother."

Introductions concluded, Clement lowered himself back into his chair. "How is he by the way?" he asked them. Then without pausing answered his own question. "Still a wastrel I suppose, frittering away his talents in that ridiculous Library?" Adam tried to keep a neutral expression, although he was pretty sure he could see at least one obvious family trait. Both Bombast and Clement seemed extremely keen on the sound of their own voice.

"It's not a normal business-related query we wanted to discuss with you... or at least not exactly," Lucid informed him, ignoring the question about Bombast. "We have been asked to look into some... unusual occurrences that have taken place in and around Moonshine recently and I wondered if you had seen anything odd, anything out of the ordinary in your time here?" Clement's amiable façade froze for a moment and his voice was noticeably less friendly than before when he spoke. "Nothing I am afraid, or at least nothing more unusual than is normally the case around these parts. I am afraid you gentleman have made a wasted journey."

"Isn't there anything you can think of that would help?" Adam asked. "You have seen the strange Sleepwalkers in and around Moonshine?" Clement nodded very slightly as Adam continued. "I know it might be a coincidence, but the timing of their appearance is almost exactly the same as the opening of the new Chimera building."

At this Clement's expression went from neutral to stony, his eyes darting from side to side for a moment with a slightly hunted look before he answered Adam. "I don't know what you are suggesting, but I am afraid I can't help you."

"But..." Adam began, before Clement cut in again. "I am very sorry, but I cannot listen to this kind of objectionable talk, I must ask you to leave," pressing a small button on the side of his desk as he spoke. Within a few moments a door at the back of the office opened and a pair of figures walked through, dark silhouettes resolving themselves into two rather unpleasant characters as they entered the light of the office. "Chimera values its reputation very highly and I wouldn't like to think you would be going around spreading nasty, unsubstantiated rumours." Clement indicated across to the two new arrivals, still stood silently by the door. "These two gentlemen are my colleagues Mr. Twitch and Jingle. They are employed specifically to make sure that our business here runs as smoothly as possible. I do hope you won't give them any cause for concern during your stay."

Adam took a moment to consider the new arrivals. They made an oddly familiar pairing, looking like an extremely nasty mirror image of Lucid and Grimble. Stood side by side you couldn't imagine two more different characters, and yet they looked entirely comfortable together, two halves of a rather terrible whole. Mr. Twitch was one of the Sornette, with their long limbs, sharp clothes, and broad grins. All of these characteristics were familiar, at least on the surface. However, as soon as you looked more closely, the differences between him and the other Sornette Adam had met were obvious and universally unpleasant.

In keeping with the style that Adam had learned to associate with Lucid and others of his race, Mr. Twitch wore a tall, slightly shabby top hat, but rather than the collection of feathers and other decorative knick-knacks that he had come to expect, this hat seemed to be circled with what looked worryingly like human teeth. Under the shade of the broad brim the eyes were hard and sharp, appearing to be on a completely different face to the broad smile that sat just a few inches beneath them. Every now and then one of the eyelids would shudder violently and the edge of the mouth underneath would twist into a momentary snarling grimace, before returning to its previous empty smile, while one of his feet tapped out a constant impatient tempo on the floor. Everything about him gave off the impression of barely contained movement, of anger and violence, likely to be unleashed at any given moment or at the slightest of provocations.

Jingle, on the other hand, was short and broad, powerfully built like most of the Drömer. He also wore a sharply tailored suit, dark material with a thin silver coloured pinstripe that matched Mr. Twitch's outfit, but unlike his partner he wore no hat. Instead his facial hair had been slicked back and a number of complex crisscrossing tramlines had been shaved into the sides. He held a short wooden club, which jangled slightly as he lovingly tapped it against his open hand. It was very similar in appearance to a Morris Dancer's stick, but somehow Adam felt it might be put to a far less pleasant use.

"I think that means we should leave," said Lucid, his voice calm, belying the slight tremor that Adam spotted in his movements as he backed away from the desk. "Thank you for your time Mr. Rapscallion, I am sure we can find our own way out."

Grimble grunted and turned sharply on his heel, casting a final withering look at the large man behind the desk before he also left, grabbing Adam's elbow, who was still staring at Mr. Twitch and Jingle, and steering him firmly out of the door with him.

CHAPTER 10

As they walked as quickly as Grimble's leg would allow down the corridor leading back from the office, Lucid was grumbling out loud to himself in a passable impression of Bombast's deep tones. "*Please treat him as kindly as you can,*" Bombast told us, "*he's just a bit weak and pompous,*" he said."

As Lucid finished Grimble spat onto the ground in disgust. "I'll tell you how kindly I would treat that idiot windbag brother of his, threatening us with his attack dogs. I'd make him wish he'd never set one of his oversized feet in Moonshine." Grimble made a rather threatening jabbing motion with his walking stick as he finished speaking.

"Who were those two?" Adam asked, as it seemed that both Lucid and Grimble had recognised the two sinister looking characters that Bombast's brother had called into the meeting.

"They are very bad news," Lucid told him, as they walked briskly across the main reception of the Chimera building, back out towards the main entrance. "As I think you gathered, the tall one goes by the name of Mr. Twitch and the other one is called Jingle. Both have a reputation for doing very unpleasant things for money, normally a lot of money."

"Of which Chimera apparently has a limitless supply," Grimble concluded for him with a scowl. "They are responsible, we suspect, for the disappearance of a number of Chimera's more outspoken critics. If you see either of them again after today then I would strongly suggest you run… preferably as fast as you can."

Adam looked down meaningfully at Grimble's bandaged leg. "I suggested that you run, not me," Grimble told him. "I will deal with them in my own way."

It took a few minutes for Lucid to arrange for the Dream-skipper to be released again from the private dock and Adam noticed that Grimble's gaze kept slipping back to the path between the docks and the Chimera company building, as if he was half expecting to see someone following them. It was therefore with a feeling of unspoken relief that they set sail away from the offices on their short journey to the city itself.

If the small Chimera dock had been an example of well-organised efficiency, the sprawling Moonshine docks were the exact opposite. It took nearly an hour for a space to be found for them, despite half of the mooring spots appearing to be available. The dock-master, who was a particularly tall Sornette wearing a horribly patterned oilskin jacket and top-hat, (also in oilskin), had spent most of the time they had been waiting arguing enthusiastically with a pair of traders who had unsuccessfully tried to unload a cargo of live giant crab-like creatures from their barge. When they finally reached some sort of agreement, which seemed to involve the Dock-master keeping one of the crabs for himself, Lucid was finally waved into an available mooring spot. The dock-master then strutted off down towards the boardwalk carrying the increasingly angry crab under one arm.

"That's not going to end well," Grimble muttered, breaking into a broad grin a few seconds later when the receding figure gave a loud yelp of pain, followed by the crab making a determined scuttling run for freedom.

As they left the Dreamskipper, wobbling down a rather rickety gangplank that had made Grimble feel queasy just looking at it, Adam took the chance to get his first proper look at Moonshine. At first glance the docks didn't look much different to the one he was used to in Nocturne, the same bustle and activity and a similar mix of exotic smells and sounds. Then he cleared the crowded boardwalk and took his first step into the city itself. The docks were on the southern outskirts of the city and as a result, led immediately into one of the more makeshift neighbourhoods. The street undulated rather haphazardly off into the distance with bits and pieces of buildings intruding into the pavement every few metres. Closest to Adam was what looked like it could have originally been a small stone cottage in the same style as those he had seen in Whimsy. However, this one had been altered so much it was almost unrecognisable. There was a brightly coloured fabric awning hanging off the front, blocking a wide section of the street and a makeshift wooden shack perched on top of the cottage roof, looking like it was getting a piggyback from the more substantial house below. Peering quickly up and down the street, many of the other buildings looked like they were also in the process of being built, repaired, extended or 'improved' in some way.

Caught up in the oddness of his surroundings, Adam was disturbed by a tap on his shoulder. "Look," said Lucid, pointing to a dreamer heading down the street towards them. Similar to quite a few others that Adam had seen, this one was half walking, half running, occasionally looking back over their shoulder at their pursuing Nightmare, but this one was quite different to anything he was used to. Rather than being a single creature or entity, this Nightmare seemed to change the entire environment around it. The street just behind the dreamer bubbled violently, as if the road itself was melting, giving off a strange and brightly coloured gas as it did so. Meanwhile, the walls of the closest buildings burst into life with violent sprays of flowers, each appearing with a tiny celebratory fanfare. The strange scene finally caught up with the dreamer a few metres in front of Adam, the bubbling pavement flipping them up into the air before they popped out of existence as they woke up back in the real world, no doubt very relieved to be away from the all the strangeness.

"Keep looking," Grimble growled. For a moment Adam wondered what he meant, as the dreamer had now gone, then it dawned on him. "The Street hasn't gone back to normal," he exclaimed in shock.

"Exactly," Grimble said with some satisfaction. "There is

something about this place which makes it more susceptible to the changes caused by dreams, good and bad. Firstly the Nightmares here are not always monsters, sometimes they are just very strange dreams where the world around you makes no sense." Adam nodded, remembering Grimble's previous warnings that Moonshine was the place where all the strangest dreams happened.

"Secondly..." Grimble continued "...as you can see the Nightmare might be gone now, but the changes to the street that it caused still remain." Looking down the street Adam could clearly see the truth in his words. The street was still uneven and scarred by a series of ridges and bubbles in the pavement, only stopping at the spot where the Nightmare had caught up with the unfortunate dreamer. Similarly, a long stretch of the wall was now marked with a line of brightly coloured flowers.

A particularly small Drömer woman emerged from a doorway within the affected section of wall and started shaking her fist angrily at the nearest bunch of flowers before trying, unsuccessfully, to stamp down some of the bubbles in the pavement outside her house. "It's one of the reasons why this place is so chaotic," Lucid said. "It's constantly changing, being rebuilt or modified, because every new dream or nightmare leaves a permanent mark."

"Like I told you... disorganised," Grimble added, sounding vaguely happy for once, having proved his point.

As they continued to make their way across the centre of the city, looking for the house where Lucid had arranged for them to stay, Adam took the chance to find out a bit more about the odd place he now found himself in. Although he was getting used to Reverie now, almost thinking of it as his second home, Moonshine was something completely new to him, fascinating and weird in equal measure. Fortunately it didn't take much encouragement for Lucid to go into full tourist guide mode.

"Moonshine, as you see it now, started about a century ago. The whole area was filled with rogue dreams, wild uncontrolled energy," Lucid told him.

"Like we just saw around that dreamer?" Adam asked.

"Similar," Lucid replied, "but much, much worse. It was out of control, nothing could grow, no-one could settle here... then Deliria appeared." Lucid pointed across to the palace at the centre of the city, its towers tall and serene over the surrounding chaotic hotchpotch of houses. "She, as far as we know, is a dream being, probably the oldest one still in existence. Something about her acts like a magnet to all that wild energy. She managed to create a stable centre in Moonshine by sucking all the nearby rogue dreams directly to herself." Adam thought back to the strange objects orbiting Deliria's head the last time they had met.

"Is that what all the..." Adam made a circling motion around his head.

"Exactly," Lucid nodded. "The first groups to settle here built the palace as the heart of a new city... and Moonshine was born. It's why the area around the palace is the most stable in the city, the further you get from it and Deliria's influence the worse things can sometimes still be. These days she rarely leaves the palace, not least because whenever she does, after a while the wild dream energy comes back without her to stop it. You can perhaps appreciate what a sacrifice it was for her to come and see us, leaving Moonshine and what she sees as her responsibilities behind. For her to have kept Moonshine even vaguely under control from so far away would have been a terrible strain."

Lucid drew to a halt as they entered a new side street. "Enough sight-seeing for the moment, it looks like we are here. I managed to book us somewhere reasonable to stay," Lucid informed him. "Fortunately, for all her other oddities, Deliria is a generous employer and paid a reasonable sum up front for our assistance." Grimble made a non-committal grunt at this, although Adam noticed he wasn't so dismissive of Deliria as to turn down the offer of payment and decent lodgings. They had been able to afford something that was close enough to the centre of the city to have both relatively solid walls and a fairly normal roof. But this being Moonshine the building was still painted a very off-putting shade of purple, with the doors and windows a bright and contrasting shade of orange that hurt Adam's eyes just to look at them.

The owner of the house was there to meet them when they arrived. She was an elderly woman, who appeared to have attempted to base her own looks on a rough imitation of Deliria's. However she hadn't quite managed to pull the look off, as a result her swirling hairstyle was drooping slightly to one side, giving her the overall look of a slightly melted ice-cream cornet. She wasted no time in taking their payment, the money Lucid handed her disappearing from sight at almost magical speed. In exchange she handed Lucid a large and overly ornate key, more suited to a grand palace than a simple townhouse and with that, left them to themselves.

Adam shut the front door behind her as she left, relieved to close out the noise and overwhelming colour of Moonshine and enjoy a moment of peace and quiet. Looking out of the low window Adam could see the sky beginning to darken slightly, the strange pink mist that hung over the city fading to a deeper shade of purple as the sun sank slowly behind the taller buildings "You best make your way back to your own world soon," Lucid told him. "It will be night here shortly and you should sleep and head back to the waking world." Adam nodded, interesting as Moonshine was as a place, the constant activity, not to mention the rather unpleasant meeting at the Chimera building, had taken its toll on him more than he wanted to admit. Leaving Lucid and Grimble down in the small living room, where they had settled in for a drink and a few hands of 'Dreamers Gambit', an extremely complicated looking card game that he had tried once and then given up on completely, Adam made his weary way up to bed.

Upstairs there was a single large bedroom at the back of the first floor, with three small beds laid out against the far wall. They looked fine for Adam and Grimble, although Adam did wonder how Lucid would manage to squeeze his lanky frame onto the relatively short mattress as he settled down himself. The last thing he heard as he drifted off to sleep was the sound of Lucid laughing cheerfully, apparently having just won the first game, then sleep took Adam completely and he left Moonshine and all of its oddness behind.

CHAPTER 11

In the morning Adam sat through another awkward break-fast with Mr. and Mrs. Henson, neither one of them speaking more than two words to him, both too caught up in their own worries. Although he felt guilty, it was a bit of a relief to leave the house and head to school, although when Adam eventually got there it was to an even smaller class than the previous day and a mood nearly as dejected as that of the Henson's home. Half of his classmates were now off with the mystery illness that was sweeping the town and judging by the news report that he had heard in the background when he had been eating his breakfast, the same thing was taking place all over the Country.

Miss Grudge had put a brave face on things and had been un-usually tolerant of Adam's distracted state. A couple of times she had even looked slightly worried, although Adam quickly discounted this as his tired brain playing tricks on him. As a result, and very unusually for Adam, he made it to lunchtime without suffering any major mishaps or earning a detention. This meant he was able to eat lunch with the rest of the school rather than sit alone in the classroom, as he seemed to do most of the time recently. With pretty much half the school missing, the dinner ladies had taken to overloading everyone's plates with extra mashed potato just to use up all the left-over food. Looking at the beige and lumpy mounds of mash, piled high on his classmate's plates he breathed an inward sigh of relief that he had a packed lunch instead.

Not feeling particularly sociable he made his way to an empty table in the corner of the hall and sat down to eat. He had just started when he was disturbed by Nora's arrival, who wasted no time in shuffling into the seat opposite his. "Uh... hi," he managed, through a mouthful of crisps. "How are things? I mean after getting chased by that dog... and um... everything." Adam took a quick look around as he spoke, but it looked like they were far enough away from the other kids to not be overheard.

"I'm fine... but that's not what I wanted to talk about, not exactly anyway. I have been thinking a lot since we last spoke and I think I might be able to go there with you... back to the dream world I mean," Nora told him awkwardly. "I'm pretty sure that Mittens knows a way. She made the journey from Reverie to this world after all... and I think that she could help me go back there." Adam stared at her open-mouthed, then he remembered himself and managed to re-arrange his face into what he hoped was a slightly more normal expression. It was certainly not how he would have expected a normal lunchtime conversation to start, but it seemed like every conversation he had with Nora was going to be full of surprises and about as far from normal as you could get.

Despite this he had to admit he was very tempted by what she was suggesting, things in both worlds were getting increasingly difficult to cope with. Charlie, who he had relied upon so heavily last time he had faced troubles in Reverie, was still laid up in bed, with an illness he was increasingly suspicious had something to do with the strange things going on in the dream world. And in Reverie he felt that things were slipping away from him too. He was no closer to finding out what was causing the strange Sleepwalkers and he was feeling increasingly distracted by the painfully slow drip-feed of information about his parents.

"It's not all that safe there at the moment," Adam said to her. "There's some weird stuff going on... again."

"I know," Nora replied, but with more determination in her voice this time. "I have seen the odd things going on here too, everyone at school getting ill all of a sudden. I'm not an idiot and I can put two and two together. There is something bad happening again isn't there?"

Adam couldn't really deny it, so simply nodded in agreement. "Yes... or at least I think so," he admitted. "But I haven't got a clue what's actually going on there... or why it seems to be affecting people in this world."

Nora shrugged, "It doesn't matter, we can work it out between us. You might have had to save me last time I was in Reverie, but this time I want to do something to help."

Adam scratched the side of his nose absentmindedly as he turned Nora's offer over in his mind, then quickly stopped himself and lowered his hand, feeling suddenly self-conscious as she stared at him waiting for his answer. "Okay," he said, "if you really think you can get back to Reverie. But I thought you said that Mittens didn't want to go back there?"

There was a rushing liquid sound that Adam was starting to recognise and Nora's eyes filmed over as Mittens spoke for a moment. He quickly looked around the School Hall again, worried that someone might notice, but Nora was sat facing in towards him, so only Adam was able to see her face. "You are quite right," she told him, now in Mittens' scratchy tones. "I didn't want to go back, but I keep getting these strange feelings that I am not used to having. I feel like there are things I need to do, I am concerned about what is happening to people, like your friend Charlie. I do not like these feelings, they are not normal, and certainly not usual for me." She scowled and then sighed, a strange rasping noise. "So it seems the only way I can deal with things is to help you. Nora is right, I do know a way back to Reverie and I think I can take Nora there with me."

"So what do you suggest?" Adam asked.

"We both try and enter the Great Dream tonight," Mittens replied. "You go there your way and I will take Nora to Reverie in mine. I will find you easily enough. That's something that I am particularly good at." She grinned slightly unpleasantly, showing a set of teeth that for a moment looked longer, and possibly a little bit pointier, than normal.

Adam tore his eyes away from her teeth and focused back on

the slick black eyes. "Fine," he replied, "then I suppose I will see you tonight."

Mittens smiled again. "It's a date."

"Yes... I mean no, obviously not... um see you later then." Adam muttered before grabbing the rest of his uneaten lunch, stuffing it back into his bag and standing up rather hastily, banging his knees painfully on the underside of the table as he did so. Although he didn't speak to Nora again for the duration of the afternoon's lessons, he couldn't quite shake the image of Mittens' pointy grin from his mind.

✳ ✳ ✳

That night it took Adam rather longer to get to sleep than normal, despite how tired he was feeling. The thought of entering Reverie with someone else was proving more awkward to come to grips with than he expected. His earlier feelings that it would be nice to share his experiences and adventures with someone from his own world, someone that would understand, were starting to fade. Oddly the main thing he was feeling now was... jealousy. Up until now the dream world had been something that was unique just to him. While he had tried to keep a level head about things, it had been exciting to be the hero of Reverie, the lone Daydreamer. Now Nora was going to be there too. When he did finally drop off to sleep his brow was creased with unexpected worries.

CHAPTER 12

Back in Reverie Bombast was also worried, which was not a feeling he was particularly familiar or comfortable with. He was sat on a high ridge some distance from the Stairway of Dreams looking out across the valley that surrounded it. Although the area around the Stairway was still stained with the damage caused by the Horror that Adam and his companions had narrowly defeated a few weeks before, in some places the lush greenness of the surrounding land had begun its slow return, gradually erasing the more distant signs of their battle. However it was not this, nor the curved strands of the Weave that encircled it, that drew his attention or were the cause of his concern. Rather it was the mass of figures, tiny and ant-like at this distance, that were making their way towards the Stairway in long, steady, snaking lines.

Earlier in the day Bombast had taken the chance to get a closer look, moving with a quiet and assured stealthiness that would have amazed Adam had he seen it, a world apart from the flamboyantly loud character that he would have expected based upon his visits at the Library. It hadn't been a huge surprise to Bombast (nothing ever was) when he had seen that the mass of slowly walking figures consisted entirely of oddly vacant looking Sleepwalkers, their skin tinged with an unhealthy green pallor, their eyes unfocused. However, despite the apparent lack of awareness of their surroundings, every one of them was moving without pause or deviation towards the Stairway, joining the increasing throng of gently swaying men, women, and children that already surrounded the base of the stairs.

The gathered figures didn't appear to be doing anything

other than standing there, with more and more arrivals increasing their numbers by the minute. Despite this Bombast could feel a growing sense of pressure, of something undoubtedly wrong about the scene laid out below him. He finished scribbling a note on a small rectangle of thin paper, which he then carefully rolled into a tight cylinder before placing it gently into the message tube strapped to the leg of Roger, his favourite carrier pigeon. "Off you go then little fella," he muttered, giving the nervous bird a final re-assuring stroke, and with that he released it into the air. Within moments it was just a speck in the sky and then even that speck was lost to sight. Bombast settled back down to watch the scene below, fingers twisting the pointed end of his beard with unusual nervousness.

CHAPTER 13

Adam had picked a spot close to the centre of Moonshine to appear when he awoke back in Reverie, a small paved square that he had noticed on his previous walk around the city. He had thought it better to arrive somewhere away from where Lucid and Grimble were staying and then take the time to introduce Nora to them more gradually, rather than just appearing with her without any explanation. Explaining Mittens was going to be quite tricky enough, and if he was honest with himself, he was quite happy to put off that moment for as long as he possibly could. The spot he had picked seemed perfect, secluded and therefore somewhere he was less likely to draw attention to himself as he blinked into existence. Unfortunately for Adam it seemed the last time he had seen the square hadn't been at all typical of its normal use.

As he woke and blearily looked around, the first sensation he experienced was a sharp pain in his back, the second was the sound of a woman's shrill scream. Jerking upright in a sudden panic he looked around trying to work out what was going on. He was immediately confronted with a wide and very heavily made-up woman's face, screwed up in a look which mixed surprise, shock, outrage and then a bit more surprise for good measure. Currently she was inhaling deeply, presumably powering up for another huge scream.

"Whoa... take it easy!" Adam managed, trying to look as unthreatening as he could and attempting to work out what was going on at the same time. There were several clues to help. Firstly he was higher off the ground than he should be, secondly the cause of the sharp pain he had felt turned out to be a rogue spoon jabbing into his back. Finally, and most conclusively, just by looking around it was immediately obvious that he had appeared directly on the top of a large dinner table. To one side there was a bowl of overturned soup, some of which appeared to have spilled onto the lap of the unfortunate screaming woman. To the other side was a large plate of something which looked similar to pasta, although in this case with Adam's foot currently resting right in the middle of it. The owner of the pasta was a man with outlandishly large mutton-chop whiskers and thick-rimmed glasses, which he was currently rubbing in disbelief.

Muttering a series of scarcely audible apologies Adam pushed himself off the table, trying his best not to cause any more damage as he did so. Once he was clear of the table and back on his feet he had the chance to look around properly. The courtyard was full of similar looking tables, although generally much tidier than the one he had just left. Taking the chance to stammer one final apology to the red-faced woman, who was still inhaling for what was promising to be one of the greatest screams of all time, he turned and walked calmly out of the courtyard. Then he ran... really, really fast.

A couple of minutes later he was leaning, panting heavily, against the wall of one of the local cafés, relieved to have escaped the scene of his previous embarrassment. However before he had the chance to enjoy his reprieve, this moment of peace was disturbed by an amused cough from just behind him. "Nice work... I can see now how you got such a reputation as a hero."

Adam lifted his head and looked around to see Nora standing just behind him with a broad grin on her face. "Hi Nora." Then he paused, seeing the darkness in her eyes, "Sorry, I mean hi Mittens," he corrected himself. "No offence, I'm glad you made it okay and everything, but I haven't had the best start to the day here."

Mittens just kept smiling, if anything even more broadly at the sight of Adam's discomfort. "I know," she said. "For a start, you still have some food in your shoe." Adam blushed for a moment, then grinned back at her, the ridiculousness of the whole situation too much for him to keep a straight face. "How did you find me then?" he asked.

"I told you," she answered. "I'm good at finding people, especially in the Great Dream. All Incubo are, and besides... that Lady who you nearly landed on screamed really, really loud."

"And Nora?" Adam asked, "Is she there with you, is she awake in Reverie now?"

"Of course," Mittens replied, seeming slightly affronted by the question. "Now we have all met up safe and sound I can hand things back over to her."

"Catch you later Adam," she added with a wink, after which the darkness disappeared from her eyes.

When she spoke again it was back in Nora's voice. "So this is what all the fuss was about." Her eyes widened with fascinated surprise as she looked from side to side, taking in all the sights of Reverie. "This place... it's amazing." Adam nodded, although briefly taken aback by her enthusiasm, he remembered that Nora had never seen the dream world outside of her time trapped within the nightmarish Horror. As a result she had only ever seen the very worst that the world had to offer. All of the things about the dream world that he loved and had come to take for granted were completely fresh and new to her. The smiling faces of the inhabitants, the easy conversations between the groups of lanky Sornette and the stocky Drömer, the outlandish buildings, even the odder and less threatening examples of Nightmares popping into existence as they walked through the streets of Moonshine, brought new gasps of delight from her.

As they walked through a narrow alleyway, which linked the main street to the road with their rented house, one of the Nightmares appeared almost directly in front of them. This one settled into the shape of a large moth-eaten teddy bear, half-heartedly pursuing a small elderly lady who was making a spirited, but very slow, attempt to run from it with the aid of two walking sticks. The old lady passed them, ignoring them completely, fully concentrating on escaping her bad dream, but the Nightmare slowed (even more) as it reached them and then stopped completely. It sniffed the air for a moment, before turning to face them with a look of confusion on its face. Then it leant in towards Nora, who looked panicked for a moment, before her expression cleared and her eyes narrowed, filling once again with blackness. Rather than backing away any further, Nora pushed her face in towards the Nightmare and she hissed menacingly, producing a quite inhuman sound. The nightmare teddy recoiled in surprise and lowered its head, before quickly turning away and shuffling off after the old woman, who had used the delay to gain a few metres lead on her pursuer. Adam and Nora both stared as the odd couple very slowly made their way off into the distance and around the corner at the end of the alleyway.

"That was... unusual," said Adam. "I've not seen a Nightmare acknowledge anything or anyone other than their dreamer before."

Nora shrugged uncomfortably. "I'm pretty sure that they can sense Mittens. She can definitely feel the presence of other Nightmares, although fortunately most of them seem to be a bit scared of her."

"You're definitely full of surprises," said Adam. "But for the minute let's just get across the city and find Lucid and Grimble. They are going to be surprised enough to see you, let alone deal with the fact you have a 'friendly' Nightmare travelling around with you."

As they reached the far end of the alleyway Adam saw Nora pause for a moment, her eyes changing once again as Mittens jumped back to the forefront. She lifted her finger in warning and hissed "quiet," at Adam.

"What is it?" he whispered back, "another Nightmare?"

Nora paused, tilting her head from side to side, appearing to be listening intently to something that Adam was unable to hear. Then she stopped and shook her head. "No... not a Nightmare," she said, "something else... something worse is coming." As she said it, off in the distance Adam thought he could hear a very gentle jingling noise, a relatively harmless sound, but one that still sent an unpleasant cold feeling straight to the base of his stomach.

"What is it?" Nora asked, once again in her own voice, spotting the concern on Adam's face.

"Did you hear that sound just now?" said Adam.

"I could hear some bells off in the distance if that's what you mean," Nora replied, "but they didn't sound that bad."

Adam grabbed her arm, turning them around and facing in the direction of the rented house. "I've heard that sound before... and believe me it's not a good sound. Come on, we need to get moving," and he set off at a brisk run, Nora just behind him.

A couple of minutes later Mr. Twitch and Jingle made their way surefooted and precise down the same alleyway, the inappropriately cheerful sound of the bells which adorned Jingle's club bouncing off the walls, filling the air with the ringing.

"Jingle?" said Mr. Twitch, stopping for a moment, although his foot continued to tap, impatient to be off again, back on the hunt.

"Yes, Mr. Twitch," replied Jingle, also stopping and using the moment to catch his breath, not sharing his partner's seemingly inhuman stamina.

"I know that you like to be referred to as Jingle by virtue of your unique and admirable way of hitting people with that noisy stick of yours."

"I do indeed," Jingle conceded quite happily, running the stick along the wall, the bells running down its sides catching on the thick mortared gaps between the bricks and causing another round of jangling noises. "I like it very much, it has... gravitas."

Mr. Twitch nodded in agreement and then continued his line of thought. "And I know it causes a great deal of very justifiable fear and trepidation in the unfortunate souls we are sent to... negotiate with."

Jingle grunted in agreement, unlike Mr. Twitch he only felt it necessary to say what needed to be said and very little else. He was a firm believer in his actions speaking louder than words. Generally words like, "please stop hitting me."

"Well, it occurs to me that while it does our reputation a great deal of good, on occasion… and I mean no insult here… the noise of your jangling club does make achieving the element of surprise rather difficult."

Jingle tilted his head to one side, considering Mr. Twitch's comment carefully and eventually nodded again, seeing no fault with his reasoning. "I'll give it some thought," he said.

"Fair enough," replied Mr. Twitch, "that is all I could ask for."

"Shall we then?" he added, pointing in the direction in which Adam and Nora had frantically run a few minutes before.

"We shall Mr. Twitch," growled Jingle enthusiastically. With that the two set off again, in the steady but assured manner of experienced hunters with all the time in the world.

Meanwhile, Adam and Nora had reached the front door of the townhouse that Lucid had rented for them in Moonshine. Without pausing to knock Adam barged through the front door, which to his relief wasn't locked, then slammed it shut after Nora followed him through, turning quickly to pull across the heavy bolt that locked it from the inside. Deep down he knew that the door, the bolt and probably even the wall would be little help in stopping either Mr. Twitch or Jingle, but it made him feel slightly better all the same.

Shouting out his friend's names Adam made his way through the small house, but there was no answer, and as he reached the single bedroom located at the back of the first floor, he realised that neither one of them was there. There were however a number of worrying signs that suggested a very recent, and apparently hurried departure. In the little kitchen area there had been a plate of half-eaten food, which was out of character for Lucid, and in the bedroom one of the travelling bags had been spilled messily across the floor.

"Grimble would never be able to leave that sort of mess,"

Adam said. "He can't cope with that type of thing. I think it gives him a migraine… something has happened." He took one final quick look around the room and came to a decision. "I don't think it's safe to stay here. We need to leave… and find out what happened to them."

Less than a minute later they were back outside and making their way down the street, when a high pitched voice disturbed them. "Cooiiee… Hello young man."

Adam pivoted on the spot to see who had spoken and spotted the landlady from their earlier meeting. She was stood in a nearby doorway and beckoned to them with a crooked finger. Looking around nervously, worried that they hadn't really got time to stop and talk, Adam made his way across to her.

"Are you looking for your two friends young man?" She asked him in a hushed voice.

"Yes, have you seen them?" Adam replied, jumping slightly when he heard a jingling sound just behind him - and then feeling rather foolish as a large cat scampered past, the bell on its collar ringing softly.

"I did," she said her voice tinged with enthusiastically horrified excitement. "I came to see if you needed anything this morning and just as I arrived I saw your two friends getting into the back of one of those big steam cart thingamys. They didn't look very happy about it."

"Do you know where they went?" Adam asked, although he already had a strong suspicion.

"It had one of those Chimera symbols on its side," she told him. Her eyes were still alight, wide with the intrigue of the whole thing, "so I suppose that's where they went."

Adam nodded his thanks, beckoned to Nora and started to walk off up the street. "I do hope that your friends are alright," she called after them, trying, not very convincingly, to sound sincere. "A few times we have seen people go off in the back of one of those wagons… we don't normally see them again."

Without paying too much attention to where they were going Adam and Nora ran between several small side streets, trying to put some distance between themselves and the unseen looming threat of Mr. Twitch and Jingle. The further they got from the palace and the more organised main streets that surrounded it, the more the odder side of Moonshine started to break through. Several times they had to press themselves tightly against the nearest wall as a dreamer ran past. The most recent of these was a tired looking young man who was being pursued by a wave of cobbles that rose and fell lazily just behind him, never quite close enough to catch up with him, but never far enough behind for him to stop and rest. Despite being a result of the man's dream, the cobbles were also most definitely a real part of Moonshine, one of them catching Adam painfully on the knee as they floated by.

"Ouch!" he yelped, rubbing his leg with a grimace. "This place is altogether too dangerous. It's bad enough being chased by monsters, but now even the streets are out to get me."

"Looks to me like you just need a bit more time to get used to it," Nora replied, pointing further down the street. As the dreamer made his way down the alleyway and past other residents of Moonshine, Adam could see that they just stepped casually around him and the pursuing lumps of stone, hardly distracted from their day to day activity. An old woman buying a bag of nuts from a street vendor even reached between the dreamer and the floating cobbles to make her payment before she wandered off, noisily crunching up one of the nuts and ignoring the dreamer completely. It looked like living in Moonshine quickly taught you how to look after yourself.

The moment was broken by the unwelcome sound of gentle ringing somewhere close by. "Come on," Nora grabbed Adam's arm, "if whatever is making that ringing noise is as bad as you say then we should keep moving." Halfway up the alley, which seemed to be used as some kind of narrow street bazaar, packed with a random variety of vendors and traders using every available bit of space, there was a heavy curtain hanging between two ramshackle stalls, both selling unpleasant looking food. Once again the sound of ringing bounced down the alleyway, looking quickly around and deciding that there were no other obvious options, Nora grabbed the corner of the curtain. Pulling it slightly to one side she ducked under it, dragging Adam with her.

The sounds coming from the surrounding warren of streets were instantly muffled by the heavy material of the curtain, which also blocked out most of the light as it dropped back down behind them. Because of this it took a minute for Adam's eyes to adjust and realise that, rather than leading to another side street, the curtain had been the makeshift entrance to a small wooden shack. He jumped slightly as a dry, wheedling voice greeted them from out of the gloom. "Welcome to Madame Voyante's miraculous palace of knowledge."

Peering into the darkness Adam heard the scratch of a match being struck and a lamp sparked into life just in front of him, the sudden light making him squint uncomfortably. Directly in front of them was a small round table, shrouded in a dirty lace cloth, hanging unevenly off the edges, giving the table the look of a badly iced and rather grubby cake. Immediately behind that was a haphazardly piled heap of old, stained rags, with no sign of the speaker. Then, with a musty rustle of cloth, a face peered up shortsightedly at them from somewhere deep within the bundled material and Adam realized that what he had taken as a pile of rags was actually a person of some kind.

"You are here for a reading... to hear your future?"

"Uhhm..." Adam began, then somewhere from beyond the curtain he heard the distant muted sound of ringing working its way down the alleyway.

"Yes, we are definitely here for a reading," Nora said quickly. "A long reading... one that will keep us here for a while, right Adam?" As she finished she nudged him hard in the side.

"Yes... yes what she said," he managed.

"But I'm not sure I have anything to pay with, I think Lucid had all of our money," he added to Nora out the side of his mouth.

"The Great Madame Voyante doesn't need your money," the

bundle informed them haughtily, Adam's whisper having obviously been neither as quiet nor as subtle as he had intended. "The Great Madame Voyante foretold all, including the fact that you would have no payment with you." Despite this protestation, the little of Madame Voyante's face that Adam could see amongst the various cloths and rags that swaddled her looked rather disappointed. "Although," she added, with the slight wheedle returning to her voice, "I also foresaw that you would have something else valuable that you would exchange for my knowledge." She stared at Adam for a moment then shook her head. "No... not you," she muttered and instead turned to Nora, "but you... you have something for me."

Nora looked a bit panicked and started patting down her pockets, wondering what she could possibly have that this strange character might want. All she could find was a couple of hair slides and half a packet of mints, which she placed on the table. "I've got these?" she said uncertainly.

"Ah yes... that will do nicely," Voyante said and a skinny arm covered in thin brass bangles shot out and snatched the mints, which disappeared back within the rags alarmingly quickly.

"Right then," Voyante looked up at Adam, "I sense much that you need to be told of the future... but it is not immediately clear to me. One moment please..." She paused, and reaching up behind her head, pulled a couple of glass lenses down in front of her face. The bottle top thick glass of the lenses magnified her weak, watery eyes to double their size. As he looked into them, Adam could feel his concentration starting to drift, drawn in by the wide staring pupils.

"Hmmm... no, still not enough," Voyante muttered half to herself and lowered another two, even larger, glass discs in front of the first. Viewed through the new lenses her eyes now appeared even bigger, almost the size of saucers. It was increasingly hard to concentrate on anything other than the massive eyes, which appeared far more focused and intelligent now Adam could see them so clearly. Madame Voyante blinked for a moment and Adam managed to tear his gaze away. "Odd,"

Voyante said, "still not enough. It must be a really big foretelling that's needed here. How very strange, you don't look all that special." Adam ignored Nora's snigger as Madame Voyante reached out and grabbed a small crank handle off to one side of the table. There was a creaking noise just above them and a scattering of dust dropped from the ceiling. Then a giant lens, the size of a large serving plate, wobbled its way slowly down towards them, hanging from thick brass chains. With a final crank of the handle the lens settled into place between Adam and Madame Voyante, whose eyes were now impossibly large, blinking massively through the glass. Adam made the mistake of looking again at the dark pupils, and as he did so, the rest of the room faded away around him.

Voyante spoke again, but this time the voice was strong and clear rather than the rather weak and reedy sound that Adam expected. "Now let us see what your future holds." There was a lengthy pause, when all Adam could hear was his own breath and the only thing he could see was the dark of Madame Voyante's eye, the pupil seeming to grow ever larger until it filled his entire view. Then she spoke once again. "Your future is full of uncertainty and danger, far more than one your age should have to face... I can see a meeting in your future, unexpected and unwanted but necessary." As she spoke Adam could feel the rest of the room slipping further away from him until only her words remained. "It seems you will meet your enemy although you may not wish to, for it is the only way to learn the truth. Chimera... it is more than just an organisation, behind the name is something else, something that truly deserves the name."

"Hmmm... Madame Voyante is intrigued..." she continued, "let us see what else the mists are hiding." There was a further pause and then a deep gasping inhalation. "This enemy is one of kind... a monster, an unhappy beast, neither one thing or another and less than whole as a result." The thought of the Chimera of myth and legend flashed unpleasantly through Adam's mind, snake tail whipping around, the fangs wide and glistening as they approached him. He flinched away, raising his hands in front of his face in defence and then the image was gone, his vision cleared, and once again he found himself standing in front of nothing more than a wizened old woman wrapped in rags, the biggest of the lenses already being cranked laboriously back up to the ceiling.

"Well you are definitely more interesting than my regular sort of customer," she told him, her voice returning to normal. "Most of the time it's meeting a tall dark stranger or coming into some money, perhaps a new job." She smiled up at Adam hopefully, "I don't suppose you are coming into some money soon by any chance?"

Still shaken by the experience, the vision of the Chimera continuing to dance in front of his eyes, all Adam was able to do was shake his head as he slowly backed away, feeling the reassuring weight of the curtain behind him. "No… afraid not. Thanks for everything though," he managed to stammer, before turning and pushing his way past the hanging cloths and back into the street.

As soon as he was clear of the thick atmosphere of the odd shack he took a deep inward breath, his vision and brain both clearing almost immediately. "How about you young lady?" he heard Madame Voyante add, although her voice was now heavily muffled by the curtain, "could I interest you in a tall dark stranger or are you spoken for by that odd young man?"

A moment later Nora emerged, shouldering her way out from beneath the heavy curtain, blushing furiously. "Well that was obviously a load of rubbish," she said firmly, brushing dust from her shoulders. "Yes… definitely," Adam replied. Although he couldn't shake the memory of the giant swirling pupil of Madame Voyante's eye and the feeling that perhaps it hadn't been rubbish at all.

❉ ❉ ❉

Adam and Nora spent the rest of the day moving from place to place across Moonshine, never stopping in one spot for more than a few minutes, not knowing whether Mr. Twitch and Jingle were still on their trail. By the early evening they ended up back at a spot close to the small square where Adam had first appeared in the city and were both feeling exhausted. They found a couple of free chairs at one of the street-side cafés and tried their best to blend into the background, holding a whispered conversation. They were also hoping that the café owner wouldn't try and take their order for a few minutes, as they had no way of paying for anything.

"So what are we going to do, now we know that Chimera have taken your friends?" Nora asked Adam, her eyes darting restlessly up and down the street as she spoke. "I don't fancy their chances much," she added in Mittens' raspier tones, "unless we can get to them soon."

"If they are somewhere in the Chimera building, which I presume they are," Adam replied, "we won't even get through the front door now, let alone find our way to wherever they are being held." He sank further back into the seat, resting his head in his hands, trying to think. It seemed pretty hopeless, without Lucid and Grimble to bounce his ideas off he felt surprisingly lost and unsure of himself. Then a thought popped unexpectedly into his brain. "Maybe..." he began, "maybe there is a way after all."

Nora raised an eyebrow. "So what's the plan?"

Adam turned the idea that had just occurred to him around a couple of times in his head, checking it for weaknesses. It definitely did have its share of problems, but he was still vaguely satisfied that it had potential, so he sat up slightly straighter and explained it to Nora. "I've been into the Chimera offices before, when we first arrived in Moonshine..."

Nora nodded, "Okay... and?"

"...and if I concentrate hard enough I can normally choose

where I wake up here in Reverie, so long as it's somewhere I've been before." As he said this he saw a look of realisation dawning on Nora's face.

"Of course," she said, finishing Adam's idea for him. "So next time we come back into Reverie from our world you could choose to arrive inside the Chimera building." Then her expression darkened. "But if it's as busy as you said, surely you would be spotted as soon as you arrived. I don't see how that's going to work."

Adam sighed in exasperation. "I had thought of that," he said. "We would have to go there at night, when the building is likely to be much emptier."

"That means we would have to come back here when it's daytime in our world then?" asked Nora.

"Yes," Adam frowned, "...and it's not something I've ever tried before. I've always come here during the night when I sleep, which means it's always daytime here."

"It could work," said Nora. "But first things first, we need to get back to our world for a while."

Adam nodded, he had spotted a secluded pile of sacks, right in the darkest corner of one of the courtyards that sat behind the café. Although it wasn't the comfortable sleeping spot he might have hoped for or expected when the day had started, it looked like somewhere he could use to sleep and get back to the waking world.

"I'll watch out for you until you get to sleep," Nora told him, "then Mittens can get me back too."

Adam was surprised at how tired he felt, despite the worries of the day. "After that I suppose we will find out if the plan is going to work or not." A few minutes later and the exhaustion he felt was enough to overcome his nerves. The last view Adam had of Reverie before he closed his eyes was of Nora standing close, doing her best to keep him safe.

CHAPTER 14

Carrying out the plan proved to be far more difficult than Adam had imagined. First of all he had to arrange to be at home during the day, falling asleep at school not really being an option. That first part had been the most straightforward, he had just told Mr. and Mrs. Henson, in as weak and pathetic a voice as he could manage, that he wasn't feeling well. He felt bad about misleading them, especially when he saw the look of worry on their faces, obviously wondering if he was coming down with the same strange illness that was affecting Charlie. Still, he justified the deception to himself by reasoning that all of this was to help Charlie and all the other unfortunate dreamers who had become ill. Both Mr. and Mrs. Henson had to go to work, so after checking on both Charlie and Adam, who had stayed wrapped up in bed looking suitably sorry for himself, they left for the day.

As soon as he heard their car leave the driveway Adam was up and out of bed. Five minutes later he was out of the house and running laps of the streets closest to the Henson's house, having decided this would be the best way to make himself tired again as quickly as he possibly could. Within another half an hour he was bent over completely exhausted by the front gate, sweaty and with shaking legs, but not feeling any closer to sleep. He had realised that it was going to be hard to make himself sleepy so early in the day, but it was an essential part of his plan to get back into Reverie during the night, so he knew he had no choice. By halfway through the morning he had tried pretty much everything else he could think of. Lying in bed and letting his mind wander, counting sheep, even trying one of Mrs. Henson's Yoga and Meditation videos, but he still didn't feel tired, or at least he didn't feel the right kind of tired. Worse than that, the more aware he was of each precious moment of time slipping past, time that should be spent in Reverie looking for his friends, the more awake he felt.

He was about to give up completely when there was a knock at the door. When he opened it, it was to see an impatient looking Nora standing on the doorstep. "Where have you been?" she asked, in Mittens' harsher tones. "I have been waiting ages for you."

"I... uhm... I haven't been able to get to sleep yet," Adam replied, slightly defensively, also taking the opportunity to step across slightly to block Nora's view of the living room through the open door and the yoga video that was still playing on the television. Nora sighed, squared her shoulders and pushed past Adam into the hallway.

"Come on then," she said, still sounding very impatient and still in Mittens' voice, "we haven't got all day... or night... or whatever."

Adam found himself dragged along in Nora's wake as she strode past him and straight up the stairs to Adam's room. "Right," she said purposefully as soon as they were both in his room.

"Right what?" Adam asked, still feeling unbalanced by the combination of Nora's sudden arrival and Mittens' rather forceful approach to things.

"Do you trust me?" she asked, darkness coiling from the edge of her pupils.

"Would you be insulted if I said... not completely?" Adam managed, backing away slightly as he watched the oily blackness cover her eyes completely and start to spill out from her fingertips. He was feeling increasingly nervous about the way things were going, but as it turned out he didn't have the chance to say anything further before the coils of darkness sprang out from her hands, lightning fast, and hit him squarely in the face.

Adam opened his eyes what felt like a split second later, finding himself looking up into Nora's smiling face. It was clear that they were no longer in his room, instead the view that greeted him was that of the high ceilings of the Chimera office atrium looming above them both. "You hit me," Adam said, in what he considered was a justifiably aggrieved voice.

"So?" said Nora. "We needed to get back to Reverie and you weren't managing very well... so I helped."

"Besides," she continued as Adam stared incredulously at her, "I didn't hit you exactly, I just helped you get to sleep... very quickly."

"Fine," Adam muttered, scrambling rather awkwardly to his feet and rubbing his jaw, convinced that he was going to find a massive bruise or lump there. "Let's just do what we came here to do. The two... or three of us can talk about this later."

At night the Chimera building looked very different. Without the hubbub of activity that Adam remembered from the last time he had been in the offices, the whole place felt far more ominous. It was also much darker than during his last visit, although the main reception area was still partially lit with a series of gently glowing lamps. Each of them had a small vial of pink mist swirling below the bulb, which seemed to act as a power source for the illumination. As they got further from the main atrium the levels of lighting reduced even further and after a while, Adam found himself increasingly reliant upon Nora, who appeared to have gained inhuman night vision as one of the side effects of occasionally sharing her eyesight with Mittens. Several times during the next few minutes they were very grateful for the semi-darkness that now shrouded the building, able to duck into shadowy alcoves as a bored security patrol strolled by, idly swinging their lanterns from side to side. As soon as the patrols had gone past them, they set off again, Nora walking sure-footed and confident down corridor after corridor.

Occasionally she paused to sniff the air, then she would select their next turn. After several more minutes of this they ended up in a particularly dark passageway, with lower ceilings and more cramped walls than any they had previously explored. Halfway down there was a particularly solid looking door, slightly recessed into the wall, far more substantial than the others Adam and Nora had passed.

"This is it," said Nora, "your friends are here," indicating the heavy door. Adam looked down but couldn't see any obvious way of opening it. There was no handle that he could see, no keyhole or other opening. Nora coughed meaningfully as he continued to look around and pointed down the corridor. At the far end there was a gently bobbing light, which was spilling slowly around the corner as one of the patrolling night guards drew closer.

"I can't find a handle," he told her, increasingly desperate. Nora raised her eyebrows, glancing again towards the approaching guards.

"Then you better do something else... and quickly."

Nodding, Adam stopped his search for an opening and decided to try something else instead. Resting his hands against the heavy door, he closed his eyes and concentrated as hard as he could. He could feel the gentle warmth of the pendant around his neck as he focused his mind. Blocking the surroundings from his thoughts he tried to visualise the door, doing his best to convince the logical part of his brain that this was a dream, and therefore he could, for example, pop the door open just by thinking about it.

His mind flashed back to the hours spent practising in the grounds of the mansion in Nocturne. Lucid had met him shortly after he had woken in the dream world a couple of weeks ago with a particularly wide grin on his face and his hands hidden behind his back. When Adam had asked Lucid what he was hiding his smile had widened even further and he had brought his hands out in front of him, handing Adam the small wooden box he had been holding. Looking more closely Adam could see that the box was an intricate mixture of dark and light wood, although there was no apparent lid or means of opening it.

"What's this?" he had asked, fascinated.

"It's a puzzle box," Lucid told him, "and it will be the basis of your training today. You have shown considerable promise with your Daydreaming, managed to achieve a number of great things, but they have all been acts of force and… if I am to be completely honest, sometimes also acts of good fortune." He'd pointed to the box. "I thought it was time you learnt to apply your abilities a little bit more… delicately. Your task is to open the box without damaging either it or its contents."

"How am I supposed to do that?" Adam had asked, confused by the lack of clasps, locks or any other obvious things he could try.

"That is why it is called a puzzle box," came the reply, "the way you open it is neither simple nor straightforward… but I will certainly enjoy watching you try." With that Lucid has sat back in one of the more comfortable chairs he had pulled out from the conservatory, lowered the brim of his extraordinary top hat over his eyes, folded his hands over his lap and waited.

The box had ended up being one of the most frustrating things that Adam had ever had to deal with, the initial fascination wearing off very quickly. He had felt his way around the box as well as he could, first with his hands, and when that hadn't resulted in any success, trying a much slower and more patient search with his mind. Up until that moment everything that he had done in the dream world using his newly discovered abilities had been relatively instinctive, even the more terrifying things like his first attempt at flying, but solving the puzzle box had proved to be a very different experience. It wasn't until his third day of trying that he had finally managed to get to grips with it. He managed to get his mind sufficiently focused to feel his way around the intricacies of the box, to understand how it fitted together. Then it had been nearly another full day before he had managed to think clearly enough to start sliding the various pieces of the box around without fear of breaking anything.

On the plus side, all of the effort it had taken meant that when the final piece of the box had slid clear and the top had slowly pivoted open he had felt a sense of achievement far greater than he had expected. However, this had been almost immediately followed by confusion and then disappointment once he had looked inside the box to see what hidden treasure it contained. "A sandwich!" he looked up at Lucid accusingly. "The box was holding a sandwich... which is really old and mouldy now by the way."

Lucid just tilted back the brim of his top hat and grinned at him. "I thought you would get into the box faster, then the sandwich would have been okay. It was a really nice one too, you would have enjoyed it... if you had got into the box a couple of days ago."

Lucid left the seat where he had been lounging and wandered over to the hostess trolley, where Mrs. Snugs had placed a tray of extremely tempting looking cakes. Picking a slice that looked particularly tasty, he wrapped it up in a serviette and lowered it carefully into the box, before snapping the various mechanisms of the box closed again with several moves of his long, dexterous fingers. "Right," he told Adam, as he placed the closed box back on the table, "let's try again."

There was a loud 'Click!' and Adam blinked, the memory of the puzzle box fading from his mind and the dark corridor of the Chimera building swimming back into view. Directly in front of him the heavy door was slowly swinging inwards, the darkness within the room beyond even thicker than that of the surrounding building. "Looks like you did it, let's go," Nora hissed across to him, pointing up the corridor, where Adam could now see the shadowy silhouettes of the approaching guards, flickering unevenly in the light cast by their lanterns. Moments later they were both inside the room, with the door pushed almost, although not completely, closed. There was a tense moment as Adam and Nora both stood, hardly daring to breathe, as the patrolling guards approached the door. Then they were past and walking further down the corridor, talking casually about the end of their shift and the welcome thought of a drink and the chance to put up their feet for a while.

Once the idly chatting voices had disappeared off into the

distance Adam let out his breath in one long, relieved exhalation and took the chance to look around the inside of the room. Initially, it was too dark to see anything, but after pulling the door open slightly he was able to make out a couple of shadowy shapes against the far wall. "Lucid... Grimble ...is that you?" he said, trying to keep his voice hushed despite his nervousness. There was a muffled groan from the other side of the room that sounded a bit like Grimble, although perhaps a Grimble who had been hit very hard and was rather bruised and swollen.

"Open the door a bit more," Adam asked Nora, "I can't see."

"Fine," Nora grunted as she made her way over, "but if we get seen by the next patrol then I am just letting you know now, that it's your fault." As she pulled the door further open the darkness filling the room thinned slightly and he was able to see the two figures more clearly. Lucid and Grimble were slumped against the far wall, both looking battered and bruised as Adam got closer to them. Lucid's head was bowed and Adam wasn't entirely sure if he was conscious. But as Adam reached him he managed to lift his head and even forced a wry grin onto his face, marred slightly by the bruising around his mouth and a thin trickle of blood that ran from the corner of his lips.

"Fancy seeing you here," he croaked. "Although I am very glad to, presuming that you are here through choice, rather than as a 'guest' like us."

"How are you... what happened?" Adam asked, not really knowing where to begin.

"In all honesty... not the best I have ever been," Lucid admitted with a painful grimace. "As for what happened, perhaps I can tell you the full story later. I think for the minute it would be better to concentrate on leaving." He looked back over his shoulder. "Although I could do with a bit of a hand with that. I am a bit tied up... literally."

He managed a brief rasping laugh at his own weak joke, before he broke off into a coarse coughing fit which he struggled to control. Adam reached down behind Lucid and after a few minutes managed to loosen the rope tying his hands sufficiently for Lucid to pull them free. Moving shakily to a standing position Lucid rubbed his hands together, trying to get the blood circulating again, his fingertips pale and wrists marked where the rope had recently been tightly tied. "Grimble came off worse than me I am afraid," Lucid said. "He can be quite stubborn and Mr. Twitch didn't like that very much."

Grimble groaned again and shifted slightly, looking up with bloodshot eyes at the mention of his name. "I must be hallucinating," he muttered. "They've hit me so hard that I've started seeing idiots."

Adam smiled slightly. "Glad to see you too Grimble," he said. "Let's get you both out of here."

A couple of minutes later the four of them were making their way cautiously down the corridor. Nora was leading the way, Adam at the back and Lucid and Grimble sandwiched protectively between them. Adam had tried, very quickly, to explain what Nora was doing once again in the Great Dream, although he had skirted around the more complicated issue of Mittens for the moment, deciding that now wasn't really the time for what was sure to be a very difficult conversation. In more normal circumstances it was clear that both Lucid and Grimble would've had many more questions. Lucid in particular kept darting questioning looks in Nora's direction, but the events of the last day had obviously taken their toll and for the moment they just seemed glad to be out of the cell. Despite repeated offers of help Grimble was insistent on making his own way down the corridor and had requisitioned a broom, which he had snapped to a more usable length and now served as a makeshift crutch, the bristled end tucked rather uncomfortably under his arm.

They had just reached the atrium and the promise of imminent freedom when Nora stopped suddenly, raising her hand to the others, although it was Mittens' voice that emerged once again from her mouth. "Over there," she said, pointing to a corridor on the opposite side. "There is something over there, something important."

Adam looked between her and the battered figures of Lucid and Grimble and sighed to himself, realising that his night wasn't over yet. "Fine… can you two go to the palace?" he said to Lucid and Grimble. "Speak to Deliria and let her know what has happened."

"How about you?" Lucid asked.

"We will meet you there, but I need to check what it is that… Nora has found first. We might not have the opportunity to get into Chimera's offices again, I can't waste the chance."

"If you must," Grimble muttered, obviously struggling with the idea of leaving Adam and Nora, but also aware that he was only just about capable of standing at the moment. "But don't be long."

"Stay safe," Lucid added, giving Nora one last probing stare before the two of them made their way, slowly and painfully to the building's exit, leaning on each other like a pair of broken, mismatched bookends.

As soon as Adam saw them leave, which left one of the main doors in a rather worse state than before, he wasted no further time in following Nora. She had made her way to a corridor on the opposite side of the atrium and as he caught up with her, Adam could feel the atmosphere around him change. The air was thicker and muggier the further they walked and there was a strange mix of smells hanging heavily around them. Oddly there seemed to be no guards, or any other staff, in this part of the building. This made their progress more straightforward but left Adam feeling increasingly worried as to why this area was so quiet.

From a few metres ahead Nora called back softly, but with excitement clear in her voice. "This is it," she said, resting her hand against the door at the end of the corridor, "up ahead is whatever it was that Mittens could feel. Whatever is going on in Moonshine is behind this door."

CHAPTER 15

Taking a deep breath, Adam pushed against the door and wasn't completely surprised when nothing happened. "It's locked," he hissed to Nora, who just shrugged.

"Just do that thing you did before, you know the…" she made a vaguely mystical swirling motion with her hands. Whether it was because he had just managed it on the cell door a few minutes before, or because there wasn't the same imminent risk of an approaching guard to deal with, this time Adam found he could open the lock of the door almost without thinking. All he had to do was convince his brain that this was his dream, and in his dream the door was definitely not locked. Once his brain accepted that fact the rest of the world seemed to fall into line.

As the door slowly swung open a pink glow filled the corridor around him, seeping through like a slightly sickly sunrise. Adam stood for a moment, drinking in the odd surrounding sights, sounds and smells on the other side of the doorway, trying to make sense of it all. The room they had entered was huge, cathedral-like in scale. Unlike the rest of the building the roof was high and domed, sitting over two large open pools, both of which contained a swirling mass of the misty substance that Adam recognised straightaway as the Weave. To one end of the domed room there was an opening that fed into the larger of the two pools and through which the slow boiling churn of the Weave entered the chamber. The location of the building on the banks of the Weave made more sense now, and although he didn't fully understand what he was seeing, a few pieces of the puzzle started to slide into place in Adam's mind.

The Weave contained within the smaller of the pools was

stained an unnatural pinkish colour, presumably also the source of the glow that filled the room. The coil and twist of it looked somehow less healthy than that of the larger unstained mass in the bigger reservoir and although Adam didn't immediately know why, his stomach tightened at the sight of it. His mind flashed back to the lanterns he had previously seen lighting the grand foyer of the Chimera offices. The small glass vials of pink gas he had seen and ignored at the time meaning more to him now. The strange effluvium cart he had seen in Nocturne also came back to mind and he was pretty sure he could remember seeing at least one glass canister full of the same odd gas on that as well. Unpleasant realisation filled his brain.

"That's how Chimera power their technology," he said to Nora, "they use the Weave." He paused and swallowed heavily, trying to get rid of the sudden metallic taste in his mouth, remembering what Lucid had told him when he'd stood on its shores for the very first time. *"Every dream that ever was and ever will be comes from the Weave… and eventually returns to it."*

"They are using dreams as fuel." He thought of dream beings like the Lady, who returned to the Weave when their time in the world came to an end, expecting a peaceful eternity floating amongst the mass of other dreams. A feeling of sick anger grew within him as he looked back at the corrupted pink mist. Now he understood its unnatural movement. He realised with a sharp, rigid certainty that the Weave was in pain.

The angry tumult of his thoughts was disturbed by the sound of a gate slamming down behind them, blocking the door they had used to enter the chamber, and a second quieter and more distant sound as another door at the far end of the room slid smoothly open. The unmistakable figure of Clement walked out onto the platform which jutted out between the larger reservoir and the smaller pool containing the treated pink mist. For a moment he looked slightly uncomfortable, and then the slick and businesslike persona that they had come to recognise settled back over him.

"When I was told that someone had entered this facility

without invitation, and at such an unsociable hour, it didn't take a genius to work out that it would be you," he sighed, sounding genuinely regretful. "So now you can see what we are doing here, what we are achieving." He held his hands out to either side, taking in the surroundings, his voice carrying easily to them despite the distance, reflected off the dome of the building's roof. He even managed to tease a weak smile onto his face as he spoke, still maintaining his amiable front despite the threatening atmosphere that Adam could feel growing in the room.

This feeling of impending danger was increased considerably with the arrival of the twin figures of Mr. Twitch and Jingle, presumably summoned by Clement, like a pair of extremely unwelcome, psychopathic genies. They had arrived either side of the spot where Adam and Nora stood, slipping through two further doors in the far wall and approaching slowly along the narrow walkways which ran in a circle around the larger reservoir. For the moment they were still some distance away, but Adam knew that it was only a matter of minutes before they reached them.

"We knew that the Weave was a potential source of energy," continued Clement. "All those dreams just floating around, not doing anything... not being used for anything." As he spoke he reached down into the reservoir with an odd device that looked a bit like a giant pair of tongs, pulling a strand of the Weave out from the swirling mist. He held it out at eye level, examining it critically for a moment. "And we were right," he said. "There was energy in the Weave, but to be completely honest with you we really needed more. There is so much we have achieved, so many machines to power, so many advances to make, and I am afraid that the unrefined energy of the Weave just wasn't enough." He walked over to the second smaller reservoir, where the mists were stained the strange pinkish colour. Reaching out he released the strand of Weave held within the Tongs. For a moment Adam thought that the wispy strand of mist wasn't going to drop, seeming to have wrapped itself firmly around the tongs, then Clement shook his hand and it dropped into the pink mist below. As it touched the surface it coiled and writhed violently for a moment, before its colour changed to match the rest and it sank slowly into the mass below.

"Then we discovered this," he said in slightly hushed tones, although the shape of the room meant that his words still easily reached Adam and Nora's ears. "With the right treatment you can turn it into something far more potent."

"You shouldn't do that, it's not right," Adam said, his voice laced with anger. "It's not natural, it's hurting the Weave and it's hurting the people that come here to dream."

Clement sighed, and when he spoke again he did so slowly and calmly, as if he was trying to explain something very simple to a small child. "This is progress. We will revolutionise the way that things work here in Reverie, make life better."

Adam thought of Charlie, laid up in bed, his face pale and streaked with sweat, eyes red with exhaustion and fever. "It's not making life better, it's hurting people... it's making them ill. You've seen the strange Sleepwalkers. Every one of those is someone who is ill back in my world... and you, you are doing it to them."

Clement shook his head. "No," he said, at first hesitantly and then increasingly firmly. "I have been told, the side effects of our work here have all been dealt with. It's safe, completely and utterly safe. Every major scientific breakthrough has its own challenges, obstacles to overcome."

Adam felt Nora nudge him in the ribs and tore his gaze away from Clement, instead looking across to his right-hand side following the line of Nora's pointing finger. Mr. Twitch had been working his way steadily around the walkway towards them while Clement had been talking, and was now no more than fifty metres away. To his other side he heard a gentle ringing noise and he risked a quick look to his left. The squat, menacing figure of Jingle was silhouetted against the gentle lighting in the chamber, a similar distance away.

"Don't come any closer," Adam shouted, pointing first to Mr.

Twitch and then to Jingle. "I'm warning you... stay back." His voice bounced off the curved walls and ceiling and when it returned to his ears it sounded shaky and nervous. "Can you see another way out," he muttered to Nora, keeping his voice as low and quiet as he could.

"Sorry," Nora replied, "but the door behind us looks like it has been sealed shut, even your weird mind powers might struggle to open it again in a hurry. It looks like the only way out is to get past one of those two. Her eyes slicked over for a moment and when she spoke again it was in Mittens' voice. "So which one of them are we going to try and go through? I think Jingle might be the easier of the two." Adam looked at Nora's face, her previous nervous look was gone and she looked ready, even excited at the prospect of a fight, but before he had the chance to answer her the option was taken out of his hands, as Mr. Twitch suddenly burst into an unnaturally fast sprint towards them.

"Now, there is no need..." Clement began to say, but it was clear that neither Mr. Twitch nor Jingle was listening to him, any pretence of obedience gone. While it may have been a trick of the light, a reflection of the lamps or the glow of the Weave, to Adam it looked like Mr. Twitch's eyes were shining with a murderous light as he rapidly closed the distance between them. The shine in his eyes was matched by the glint of two long slim slivers of darkness which had appeared out of nowhere, one in each hand. Even at this distance there was something incredibly menacing about the dark blades, which seemed to ripple slightly as Adam stared, reminding him unpleasantly of the nightmare substance that had made up the Horror. Adam span back towards him, and fighting down any feelings of panic, concentrated as hard as he could, trying to think of a dream that would help. A memory sprang into his mind, a dream where he had felt like a giant, walking tall across the world, towering above the landscape and the tiny figures below him. He remembered the sensations that had accompanied the dream, the feeling of strength and confidence. He also tried to forget about the incredible clumsiness that had unfortunately come with it.

Eyes squeezed closed, almost immediately he could feel his body expanding and growing, matched with the familiar glow of warmth from his pendant. Opening his eyes again Adam swung his new, giant-sized arm, but as he did so Mr. Twitch had already launched himself into the air, covering the last few metres between them in one leap. This meant that rather than hitting Mr. Twitch in his chest as he had planned, Adam's newly huge arm caught one of his legs instead, flipping him around violently in the air and over the edge of the walkway.

For a moment it seemed certain that he would tumble into the swirling Weave below, but somehow Mr. Twitch managed to twist himself in mid-air, grabbing hold of the metal rail at the base of the walkway, one of his long dark blades spinning free. There was a roar of fury from behind Adam and he turned to see Jingle trying to force his way past Nora, who was now surrounded by Mittens' black tendrils which whipped protectively around her.

"No, no, no, stop all of you," he could hear Clement shouting from the centre of the chamber. "I order you to stop. I am in charge here."

Mr. Twitch had pulled himself back onto the walkway by this point and turned with a snarl. "You were only in charge because our employer allowed you to be. I have waited long enough to be let off your leash!" His arm swung in an upward arc and his remaining nightmare blade shrieked through the air almost too fast to see, although it seemed to Adam that the spinning shard changed its shape several times as it flew towards its target. Clement was still holding the large metal tongs he had used on the Weave and by sheer luck the flying sliver of darkness hit them rather than Clement himself, shattering violently with the impact, pieces of the destroyed blade pin-wheeling into the air. The force of the impact had however been enough to knock Clement backwards, and as he staggered back on unsteady feet, the look of relief on his face turned to one of panic as his final stumbling step took him over the edge of the smaller pool containing the pink stained Weave. As he fell his braces caught on one of the pipes feeding chemicals into the side of the pool and for a long and desperate moment he hung in mid-air before the elastic gave up its uneven battle with gravity. Then, with a final despairing cry, he dropped out of sight.

All of this had taken place in a matter of seconds. To one side Nora (or Mittens, or whoever she was at the moment) was still fending off Jingle, while closer to Adam Mr. Twitch was once again advancing, two more long, thin nightmare blades appearing as if by magic in his hands. "Oh come on, seriously, where does he even get them all from?" Adam muttered to himself, bracing himself to attempt another daydream, maintaining the giant version of himself having been too much effort to manage for long.

As he did so he heard a shout of distress from Nora, looking quickly back over his shoulder, he saw her slumped over. A jubilant looking Jingle was advancing on her with his club raised, although she was making a spirited attempt to crawl away, it was clear she wasn't going to escape him. "Nora!" Adam shouted, all thoughts of self-preservation gone from his mind, turning his back on Mr. Twitch despite the danger. He felt a familiar glow of anger growing in his chest at the sight of Nora's prone form and almost without thinking he brought his hands together to create a shockwave of dream energy as he had in the past.

As he did time seemed to slow around him, and as his hands drew closer together, it felt like he was trying to swim in a pool full of treacle. During that incredibly long moment he thought that he could see the glow from the giant pool containing the Weave intensifying, seeming to react to his actions. As his hands met the resulting blast was far greater than anything that Adam had ever previously experienced, geysers of mist bursting from the surface of the Weave in violent eruptions. The domed ceiling of the chamber shuddered as the pressure in the room grew, and then with an unbelievably loud splintering noise a giant crack appeared in the roof, running from end to end, turning the previously solid structure into an unstable mass of overhead crazy paving.

Before Adam had the chance to finish wondering whether he had maybe gone a bit too far, chunks of the roof were plummeting towards them, crashing into the reservoir and causing waves of mist to cascade onto the walkway, which was now also shaking unsteadily. Several of the rivets which held it in place shot across the room, ripping clear of the wall and pinging across the room like bullets. Rather too late Adam remembered that his powers seemed to be intensified by proximity to the Weave, or at least that the Weave seemed to react to whatever he did. Either way he had released something much, much more potent than he had intended. Then a small chunk of the falling masonry caught the side of his head with a glancing blow as it came down, knocking him flat on his back, precariously close to the edge of the misty reservoir.

Exhausted and battered, his head aching from the sudden blow, Adam could feel everything starting to fade, the temptation to sleep and escape it all too strong to resist. In the background he could still hear the sounds of the building tearing itself apart and he knew that his friends still needed him, that he couldn't afford to let his eyes close, but it was getting increasingly hard to concentrate. Just as he felt he couldn't hold on any longer, ready to let the warm comfort of sleep take him away, he felt a strange sensation washing over him.

Forcing his eyes back open, he saw that some of the Weave had washed up out of the pool and gathered around him, the misty tendrils wrapped gently around his outstretched arms. As he lay there he thought he could hear a soft voice, a quiet but persistent whisper on the very edge of his hearing, trying to get his attention. "Adam... Adam stay awake... be strong." He was so disoriented that he couldn't tell if he was really hearing anything or if he had just become delirious, but even in his current state the soft voice was instantly familiar and comforting. He managed to push himself up onto his elbows and raise his head slightly and was met by an impossible sight. Directly in front of him the surface of the Weave was bubbling and churning and as he stared, it rose gently swirling into a shape he immediately recognised.

"Mum?" Adam croaked, reaching out a shaking hand.

"Adam," the soft voice replied inside his head, and the softly wavering figure formed from the mist held out a hand to match his, fingers open and outstretched. As the figure's hand touched his, palm to palm, his fingers interlaced with the misty digits and he felt a rush of warmth and recognition. The voice in his head returned, stronger than before and while the misty figure in front of him had no real features that Adam could see, in his mind he could clearly picture his mother's face. Her eyes were warm and surrounded by gentle lines, carved out through years of laughter, her mouth smiling and proud.

"You have done so well Adam," the voice told him. "You have been so brave. I know you are tired and want to rest... but your friends need you... Reverie still needs you." As the voice echoed in his head Adam could feel some strength returning to his exhausted limbs, as if the touch of the Weave was energising him.

"Mum," Adam repeated, "is that really you? Where are you? ... How are you? ... I miss you."

The gentle touch of the Weave on his hand tightened for a moment in a reassuring squeeze. "I'm fine," his mother's voice said. "I have been watching over you and I am so proud of what you have become..." The voice paused and the Weave figure turned to one side, as if it had been disturbed by something that Adam couldn't see. "I have to go," the voice said with sudden urgency. "Stay strong Adam..." At this, the Weave figure lost its substance and the swirling mist dissipated. For a moment Adam could still feel the touch of the hand on his, then it was gone and his fingers closed on empty air. The strange sense of unreality passed and time seemed to catch up with him, the surrounding sights and sounds all crashing back into focus at once. The metal walkway was bucking unsteadily under him, the air full of dust and cries. The tiredness that he had previously felt was entirely gone, leaving Adam feeling as strong as he could ever remember. Wasting no time he grabbed hold of the nearest railing and dragged himself back onto his feet.

As he did there was a final resounding cracking noise and a huge piece of the ceiling came loose directly above them all. He saw Jingle staggering back away from Nora's collapsed form, eyes on the ceiling and without thinking Adam ran forward and threw himself protectively over her. His mind flashed back to when he had saved her from the Horror, cocooned safely within a protective shield of glowing dreams. Without fully under-standing how he had managed it, he once again wrapped them both in as much energy as he could muster. Split seconds later the whole ceiling came crashing down and everything around Adam went dark, his vision fading to a tiny, painful pinprick of light.

CHAPTER 16

Rather than waking immediately back in his own world, when his vision cleared Adam found himself in an unexpected yet familiar place. As soon as his mind adjusted to the fact that he was not yet home Adam recognised the scene immediately. The plain, worn wooden bed, the slightly ruffled bedclothes and the face of the young sleeping boy lying still and serene. He realised he'd found himself in the presence of the Dreamer as he had once before. The boy who the inhabitants of Reverie believed had imagined the whole place into existence. A feeling of tranquility washed over him, the hectic and violent memories of the Chimera factory relegated for the moment to the back of his mind. Then his vision jerked queasily and the fleeting peace and serenity that he had felt dropped out from under him. When his vision settled again he was now next to the sleeping figure, much closer than he had been before. As he stood, almost within touching distance of the boy, he could see a single small bead of sweat on the sleeping child's forehead. Despite its tiny size, the bead of sweat looked completely out of place to Adam, incredibly wrong. Then everything around him swam out of focus once again and the scene was gone.

Adam sat upright with a sharp gasping inhalation of breath, finding himself back in the spare room at Charlie's house. Rather than waking in the bed as he normally did, he was sprawled awkwardly on the floor. He climbed rather painfully to his feet, then the memories of the most recent events in Reverie came flooding back, hitting his brain like a tidal wave, and he nearly fell over again. He looked around for any sign of Nora, but couldn't see her anywhere. As she wasn't here with him he desperately hoped that she had awoken back at her house, but he couldn't stop his mind playing through all the worst possibilities that he could think of.

Even running as fast as he was able it still took him nearly half an hour to get round to Nora's house. By the time he arrived he was exhausted, leaning against the front door and trying to draw his breath as he rang the doorbell. As a result, when the front door suddenly opened he stumbled forward and ended up face down on the thick brown carpet of the hallway. "Hello Adam," said a very welcome voice.

"Hi Nora," he managed from his prone position, so pleased she was okay that he was able to ignore the embarrassment he felt sprawled awkwardly on the floor.

"So that was Reverie then," Nora said to him, sat at the kitchen table in her parent's house a few minutes later. "Interesting place... although it looks like I'm never going to have a normal visit."

Adam grinned sheepishly. "The place can be nice, honestly. You've just been unlucky so far..." He paused seeing Nora's expression, "...really, really unlucky."

"So what do we do next?" Nora asked him. "I mean, it looks like we know what is causing all the problems in Moonshine now, and most probably what is making people ill here too. But you destroyed the factory, so does that mean it's over?"

Adam shook his head. "I can't believe that's all there is to it. Those thugs were working for someone else, not Clement. And I didn't actually mean to destroy the factory... although I am glad that I did."

Recent memories of the contaminated Weave rose again in his mind, the misty strands writhing uncomfortably. "What they're doing isn't misguided, it's evil. We can't let them carry on... and I think that the illness that they are causing is doing something even worse. I saw the Dreamer again, just for a moment before I woke up back here and... I think he was ill too." He knew that Nora wouldn't completely understand, she had never seen the Dreamer, but he also knew without a doubt that something incredibly wrong was happening. "I don't know what would happen if the Dreamer got ill, but everyone believes he is the creator of Reverie, so I am pretty sure it would be terrible for the dream world and everyone in it."

Looking out of the window Adam could see the sky starting to darken slightly as the sun began its slow descent. Although he had been asleep for much of the afternoon, spending his time in Reverie, the excitement of the events that had taken place, and the following worries about Nora had still left him tired.

"Are you okay to come back to Reverie again tonight?" he asked Nora. "I know you haven't had the best of luck with your visits so far, but you were really helpful last time and..." he paused and drew a deep breath, thinking of an appropriate compliment he could pay her. Unfortunately his brain, normally a reliable source of any number of interesting thoughts, was suddenly as blank as the school whiteboard, so he ended up settling on "...and I think we probably need all the help we can get."

"Wow, thanks," Nora replied, slightly sarcastically, then grinned back across at him, the sides of her mouth turning up mischievously. "I'll be there, don't worry. It's far too interesting for me to leave things alone now."

Looking at her face, shining with scarcely contained excitement, Adam was reminded of how he had felt when he had first entered the dream world. Confused, slightly scared, but far too intrigued to do anything except let the increasingly strange events carry him along and see where he ended up. "Right," he said, making his way back to the front door. "I have to get back before Charlie's parents finish work. They think I've been ill in bed all day, so I would find it pretty hard to explain being round here."

True to her word, that night when Adam awoke in Reverie, Nora was stood there patiently waiting for him. They had arranged to meet close to the palace, where Adam hoped he would still find Lucid and Grimble. He had picked a secluded spot close to the entrance of the gardens he remembered seeing as he had passed the palace during his previous visit. This time, aside from a brief but unfortunate encounter with some brambles, he managed to arrive without too many problems. "Come on then." Nora prodded him gently once he had got to his feet and unsnagged his t-shirt from a stray thorn, and pointed across at the palace. "Let's get going."

Brushing himself off quickly Adam followed her towards the main entrance, striding straight past a pair of opulently dressed guards who, whilst admittedly looking very fancy, appeared incapable of effectively guarding anything. Never having been inside the palace, Adam was intrigued to see what it would look like, so he was a little disappointed when the main entrance hall, while grand, turned out to be pretty normal looking.

There was a high, vaulted ceiling, which matched the large pale stone slabs that made up the wide floor. To each side of them extravagant candelabras burned brightly, casting gently flickering shadows onto the stretches of white plastered wall that linked a series of tall stone pillars. The sound of their footsteps seemed unnaturally loud as they made their way to the end of the hallway, the clattering sound bouncing around the walls and high ceilings and then returning slightly out of time with their steps. As Adam and Nora approached the large, ornate doorway that framed the end of the hallway they could hear the echo of voices, Grimble's deep tones clearly recognisable despite the distortion.

Bookending either side of the opening were a pair of figures that Adam immediately recognised. The ostentatious dress, colourful ribbons and slightly stunned expressions of the two courtiers were all familiar from the first time he had met Deliria, although this time they acknowledged his approach with a friendly smile before remembering themselves and ushering them through to the throne room with a hurried, and apparently completely freestyled, fanfare. Although Adam was used to it, Nora wasn't and he could see she was trying, not completely successfully, to hide her horror at the unexpected assault on her ears. As they entered Adam spotted Deliria at the head of a table off to one side of the room, sat on a very old and comfortable looking armchair, rather than the much grander but far less comfortable looking throne, which remained empty on the dais in the centre of the room. On the other side of the table were Lucid and Grimble, who had both looked around at the horrible sound coming from the courtiers tin trumpets, first in consternation at the noise and then with delight when they realised it was to announce Adam and Nora's arrival.

"Adam!" Lucid stood as soon as he saw them, striding over to them in a few enthusiastic, bouncing, lanky steps. He leant in and hugged Adam tightly for a moment. "Good to see you, I… we were enormously worried about you both."

Grimble, although he hadn't stood at their arrival, also had a relieved expression on his face and raised his hand in greeting. "Lucid and I had just reached the outskirts of the city, making our way to the palace as we had agreed, when there was an extremely loud noise which I presume you were responsible for. We saw a huge cloud of dust rising from the Chimera building and to be honest we feared the worst, even though you have proven yourself to be surprisingly… resilient for a squishy human in the past." Adam tried to contain his smile, even when Grimble was trying his absolute best to express concern and relief it seemed he couldn't help throw in a couple of mild insults.

"We have also had a message from Bombast," Lucid told him, "an extremely worrying message, which makes our current situation even more urgent than we thought."

Adam spotted a small bird sat resting in a large gilded cage to one side of the table, a message tube tied to its leg. If it was possible for a bird to look completely exhausted, this one definitely did, its head was currently nestled in its chest and it looked like it would topple off its perch at any moment.

"So what was his message?" Adam asked, the initial pleasure he had felt at seeing his friends and their relief at his well-being rapidly eroded by the worry he could sense behind their smiles.

"It's the Stairway," Grimble told them, crossing his arms and rocking back slightly in his chair. "Bombast says that a mass of the strange Sleepwalkers is gathering around the Stairway of Dreams. He doesn't know what they are there for, but his instincts are that it's for nothing good."

Lucid leant forward, adding, "And Bombast's instincts are very rarely wrong. He knows everything that is going on in Reverie and most of the time everything that's likely to happen in the future as well. The fact he is unsure about this is troubling enough on its own."

Adam thought back to his last vision of the Dreamer and the sense of something being terribly wrong. "I saw the Dreamer again," he told them. "Last time I left Reverie I had a vision of him and…" he paused for a moment, unsure how to explain what he had felt in those brief moments, "…I felt like something was wrong… like he was ill too."

"Ridiculous," Grimble snorted. "He's the Dreamer, he can't get ill."

Deliria gave a small, polite cough, which was immediately emphasised by a loud 'dinging' sound that came from the tiny bicycle currently circling her head. "Actually Adam could be right," she said, in a quiet but firm voice. "All these unfortunate dreamers, gathering around the Stairway. All those infected dreams, building up one on top of another. It works both ways, the Dreamer created this world, but it's all of your dreams that are the lifeblood of Reverie. It's all one great cycle, your dreams, the Weave, the Stairway, all of it. If dreams become infected with something bad… it could spread… spread as far as the Dreamer himself."

Despite the ridiculous range of miniature items orbiting her head, consisting of a giraffe the size of a mouse, a pack of cards constantly shuffling themselves and a boiling kettle in addition to the still ringing bicycle, Deliria looked completely serious. It was clear her words had also got through to Grimble and Lucid who both sat in silence. Adam remembered Lucid telling him that Deliria was a dream being, one of the oldest, so whatever they might think of her, she was as close to the Great Dream as it was possible to be. Grimble in particular sat staring across at

Deliria long after she finished, his previously gruff expression slowly draining away, replaced with something much softer.

"If it is true… and much as the possibility is hard to imagine, we can't afford to dismiss it, then ending this is even more important than we thought." Lucid picked up his long frock coat from the back of one of the chairs, gesturing across to Grimble to do the same. "Thank you for your hospitality my Queen," he said, with a slightly florid bow in Deliria's direction.

"Pffft… whatever," Grimble added half under his breath and rather less chivalrously as he followed Lucid to the door. Still Adam noticed that Deliria didn't seem to be in the least insulted, smiling at Grimble's back as he stalked away, still limping and leaning heavily on a new, and very shiny, walking stick. From the ridiculously ostentatious design (the handle being in the shape of a broadly smiling and fantastically ugly unicorn) Adam presumed, quite correctly, that the stick had been provided by Deliria.

As Lucid passed Adam he tapped him on the shoulder. "You and your lady friend should come too," he told him. "I think we are all still owed a discussion about Nora's rather… unusual abilities." Adam sighed, the temporary humour of Grimble's outlandish new walking stick immediately replaced by the returning worry about how he could explain about Nora… and more importantly how… or even if, he could ever hope to explain Mittens.

CHAPTER 17

"Mr. Adam sir... Excuse me... Mr. Adam!" A well-spoken yet slightly petulant sounding voice carried across the street as Adam and his companions made their way from the palace back towards their lodgings, interrupting Adam's thoughts, which were still wrestling unsuccessfully with how exactly he was going to explain things to Lucid and Grimble. "Please Mr. Adam, if you would be so kind as to stop for a moment."

Turning on his heel rather more sharply than he had intended, with the resulting pirouette nearly unbalancing him, Adam peered across the street to see who it was trying to get his attention. On the other side of the busy thoroughfare, waving a pale hand above the throng of passers-by, was the tall figure of the snooty receptionist that Adam remembered from their first visit to the Chimera offices. Sighing to himself, pretty sure that no good would come of it, Adam signaled to the others to stop and wait as the receptionist weaved his way through the crowds, occasionally stopping with a look of undisguised horror on his face when a particularly dirty or unusual looking resident of Moonshine crossed his path.

When he reached them the receptionist was looking slightly less dapper than the last time they had seen him. A passing cart had splashed his trouser leg with mud and despite his best efforts he hadn't managed to completely avoid the crush of the crowd, leaving him rather crumpled. "Thank you, Mr. Adam. I was concerned you hadn't heard me," the receptionist blurted out, much of the pomposity from their last meeting seeming to have been knocked out of him.

"What do you want?" Grimble snapped back, glowering up

from under frowning eyebrows.

"My employer would very much like to meet with you," the receptionist managed, withering further under the combined glares of Grimble and Lucid.

"We have already experienced the hospitality of your 'employer' thank-you," Lucid replied, subconsciously rubbing his wrists, which remained sore where he had previously been tied, "and I don't particularly fancy a second visit."

"No, no, no, you don't understand," the receptionist informed them, stopping for a moment to flick hopelessly at one of the clumps of mud sticking to his sleeve with his handkerchief, "this is a business meeting, completely above board." Lucid just stared back, suspicion and disbelief clear in his eyes. "I understand that there has previously been some unfortunate... unpleasantness, the result of some over-zealous work by a couple of my employer's less disciplined staff," the receptionist continued, undeterred. "But he simply wants to talk, to explain himself."

"I don't think so," scowled Lucid.

"With respect the invitation is not to you," the receptionist told him, a little of his superior attitude resurfacing for a moment from under the flustered grime. "It is Mr. Adam here that he wishes to speak to, although you are all welcome to accompany him as far as the meeting to ensure his wellbeing."

"The answer is still no," Grimble growled.

"That is your decision of course, however should you change your mind my employer will be at the Chimera offices at noon today. He is an incredibly busy man, that he has made the time to see you is very... unusual and it is an offer unlikely to be repeated." With that parting shot the receptionist nodded curtly to them and with a visible shudder of revulsion made his way back into the crowd.

Five minutes later Adam and Nora were sat on one side of the small table in the rented house, Lucid and Grimble on the other. Lucid had poured them all another of the cups of herbal drink that seemed to be a particular speciality of Moonshine and now sat looking at Adam and Nora expectantly. "Well?" Grimble asked, looking pointedly at Nora before returning his gaze to Adam.

"It's hard to explain," Adam took a sip from his drink to try and get rid of the sudden dry feeling in his throat before he continued. "But before I start you should both know that Nora helped me to save you, she risked her life." Lucid leant forward waiting for Adam's explanation. "Uhm…" Adam could feel sweat forming on his brow. Now the time had come to explain he couldn't find the right words. "Nora has a nightmare that she wears around her wrist like a bracelet and which sometimes pops into her head, but don't worry, it's a nice one," didn't seem all that likely to win them over. He was still wrestling with the best way to start the conversation, staring down into his lap, when he heard Grimble gasp, an outraged exhalation.

As soon as he looked up his worst fears were confirmed. Nora was in full Mittens mode, eyes swimming with darkness and smiling a wide and overly toothy smile. Lucid and Grimble were both back-peddling away from the table, with Grimble rummaging in one his many inside pockets as he did so. Adam knew what was coming before it happened and grabbing a mat from the table managed to swat away the flying bag of burning herbs that Grimble launched, knocking it to the far side of the room. "No…wait!" he shouted. He turned to Mittens. "And you…" he growled at her, "you are not helping. This is difficult enough already."

"You seemed to be struggling," Mittens grinned back at him, unperturbed by his fierce expression. "So Nora and I thought this would save us all some time."

"She… she is possessed by an Incubo," Grimble stammered, eyes narrow and one hand already firmly clutching another of his bags of herbs, although Adam was relieved to see he had not lit this one yet.

"I think you better explain quickly," Lucid managed, although his voice was also cracked with uncertainty.

"She does have an Incubo with her, but she isn't possessed by it," Adam began, then stopped for a moment to go and stamp out the bag of herbs that was still smouldering in the corner. "Nora is still in control… show them Mittens, please?"

Mittens shrugged, wiggled her fingers in a cheery wave, and the blackness disappeared from her eyes like water vanishing down a plughole. When she spoke again it was back in Nora's less confident, but far more human, voice. "Adam is telling the truth," she said. "When I first told him he reacted just like you. He said that Incubo weren't to be trusted. That they were bad."

"They are," Grimble snarled back at her, still clutching his bag of herbs close to his chest like a talisman. "They absolutely are."

"I know," Nora admitted, "at least that most of them are. I have seen enough to realise that much. But Mittens is different, honestly. In all my time trapped in the Horror she looked after me, helped me cope with the loneliness. We have spoken a lot since then and she explained to me, after a while, that not all the Nightmares agree with what is happening in Reverie or with some of the things that they are being asked to do." Nora slowly sat back down at the table and looked across at Lucid and Grimble. "It would be easier if Mittens could explain to you herself. Will you let her without…" She paused and looked pointedly at the bag of herbs Grimble still held.

"Humph… fine," Grimble replied. "But if I see a single sign of anything funny… anything at all…"

Nora nodded. "Okay." There was a gentle ripple in the air and once again Mittens took Nora's place, immediately holding up her hands. "Whoa there sparky," she said, pointing at Grimble who, despite his promise, had reflexively drawn back his arm ready to defend himself. Slowly he lowered his arms, folding them across his chest instead, although still glaring at her and still with the bag of herbs gripped tight in one hand like a protective talisman.

"Go ahead then," he growled, "but this better be good."

"It is," said Mittens confidently. Squaring her shoulders she looked across the table at Lucid and Grimble and when she spoke again it was without the slightly mocking tone that Adam had come to associate with her, sounding surprisingly serious instead. "I am one of the Nightmares, true enough. As I have already explained to Adam, I do scare people. I'm good at it, I enjoy it and I am certainly not ashamed of it... it's my job after all." Grimble's eyes had narrowed, but Adam was reassured to see that both he and Lucid at least appeared to be paying attention to what Mittens was saying. "But," she continued, "recently things have been changing in Reverie. There was a natural order, we had rules that worked... and that we understood, but all that has been thrown into chaos. First Isenbard and then this 'Chimera' have been given control over Nightmares, using us like mindless tools. Some of the Incubo, myself included, don't agree with it. We miss the old ways."

"So why does that mean we trust you?" Lucid asked, leaning forward slightly across the table. His chin was resting on his hands and he looked and sounded genuinely interested rather than scared as he continued. "You are angry at the way you are being treated, but that hardly makes you our friend."

At this Mittens smiled. "True," she said, "but we share an enemy... and we also share a common goal and that makes us as close to friends as we are ever likely to be."

"And you can help us how exactly?" Grimble grunted, still looking extremely sceptical.

"I would like to think I have already proved myself," Mittens replied rather testily. "If it wasn't for me you and your tall friend would still be enjoying Chimera's hospitality." She paused for a moment, taking a moment to calm herself. "But I believe that there is more I can do, I hear things, whispers from other Nightmares. The longer I am back in Reverie the more their voices return to my ears. They say that behind the company there is something else, the Chimera itself."

"Oh great," Adam muttered to himself, "as if I wasn't nervous enough already."

Then speaking more loudly to get Lucid and Grimble's attention he added, "I know you don't like the idea, but I think I need to meet with this Chimera. Mittens has just told us that he is something different… and we need to know what we are dealing with, no matter how risky that might be." Unsurprisingly no one around the table looked happy at this suggestion, but Adam pressed on anyway. "And I was told, by this very odd fortune teller, that if I was ever to get to the bottom of what is going on, that I would have to meet my enemy… even if I didn't want to."

Grimble raised an incredulous eyebrow at this, although Adam noticed that Lucid seemed to be more willing to listen. He remembered the Maman on the Grand Barge, one of the leaders of Lucid's people, telling his fortune before and guessed that, for Lucid at least, this was something to be taken seriously.

Even with Lucid's grudging support the four of them talked around the subject for the next hour, (or the five of them if you counted Mittens, who occasionally popped up to make her opinions known, much to Grimble's annoyance). The eventual compromise being that they would all at least accompany Adam as far as the meeting. Grimble was the last to be convinced and rather grudgingly passed Adam a slim tube that reminded him a little of a stick of dynamite or a small firework, although it was a dark blue colour rather than red.

"It's something new I've been working on while I was waiting for my leg to heal. I haven't tested it fully yet, so it is only to be used in emergencies," Grimble informed him tersely. "Don't use it unless you absolutely have to, but if the worst happens then just pull the cord at the top of the tube and hold on tight."

"Why, what does it do?" Adam asked, intrigued (and a little worried).

"You're better off not knowing, it's not really designed for enclosed spaces," Grimble grunted back, refusing to be drawn any further.

Pocketing the strange tube, Adam checked the time and realising that noon was rapidly approaching, cut short any further discussion by standing up and heading to the door. A few moments later Nora joined him, shortly followed by Lucid and Grimble, although the two of them continued to hang back slightly, and several times Adam caught them staring at Nora with distrust still obvious in their gaze.

As Adam and his friends drew closer to the Chimera building, they could see it was overshadowed by the dust cloud that continued to hang over the wreckage of the destroyed dome. From a distance it looked to Adam like someone had taken a massive spoon and bashed in the top of a huge boiled egg, but as they drew closer such fanciful thoughts were quickly replaced by more serious worries. There were already signs of reconstruction and repair work. The wreckage of the dome was rapidly being cleared, with dozens of workers streaming to and from the site and a lattice of scaffold enveloping the damaged building. The small dock also seemed unusually busy, with a series of low barges, similar to those of the Sornette, constantly chugging in and out, carrying building materials. Looking more closely Adam could see the barges were all powered by engines very similar to the Effluvium carts Adam had previously seen, slim plumes of pink smoke snaking out lazily behind them.

"They will have the whole thing up and running again in a matter of weeks," Lucid muttered despondently. "How do you stop something like Chimera, they have too much money. You knock them down and they just spring straight back up again." Adam looked across at him, worried by the despairing tone. He was used to Lucid being the overwhelmingly upbeat one of their group, always smiling, always looking for the best in everything. But now his friend seemed to have had all of his normal positivity washed out of him, leaving his normally cheerful voice sounding flat and grey.

"We will think of something," Adam replied, with an optimism he wasn't sure he even felt himself. "I'll meet with whoever it is that seems to be behind all of this, see what they have to say for themselves and then we can do what we do best."

"Which is?" Nora asked, eyebrow raised slightly.

"Make it up as we go along," Adam replied firmly. "It has always worked until now," he added, spotting the look on Nora's face.

"Well that's a relief," she said, although her expression said the exact opposite. "For a minute there I thought we were in real trouble."

"I'm still not sure about this," Grimble added. "I think we can safely assume that whoever is behind all this has no fondness for you... or any of us for that matter. This is more than likely a trap."

"I know," Adam replied, looking back across at the rapid reconstruction of the domed building. "I realise that, but we aren't really any closer to stopping all this... not properly. We need to know what we are dealing with and this might be our only chance."

As they entered the building there was a noticeable increase in the number of security staff scattered across the large open foyer. Several of them glared across at Adam and his companions, eyeballing them suspiciously, which had pretty much no effect. Adam was much too nervous to really notice them anyway, his mind too full of worry about who, or what, he was about to meet. He did however notice that Nora responded to the guard's attempts at intimidation by waving cheerfully at the largest and most scary looking of the guards. He couldn't tell if Mittens had taken over again or if Nora was just getting a lot more confident. "Mittens is starting to be a bad influence on you," Adam muttered under his breath, although it was hard not to smile at the sight of her happily facing down the guards.

This time Adam was taken straight to the top floor of the office. He was escorted extremely politely and efficiently by a Sornette lady, the only nod to her heritage being a rather sparsely decorated bowler hat, topping off an otherwise severe looking business suit. To Adam, despite her apparent importance, she seemed a sad and pale imitation of the cheerful, flamboyant Sornette he remembered from the Grand Barge, with their long colourful skirts and dancing feet. The entrance to the office he was taken to was the grandest Adam had seen so far, double doors in a rich dark wood, engraved so that the pair between them displayed the Chimera symbol that Adam had become so used to, half of the circular image on each door. The Sornette lady knocked sharply once and then, without any further conversation, left Adam alone in the corridor. "Enter," a voice called from somewhere inside.

Pausing briefly to gather his courage, unsure as to what he was about to face, Adam pushed against one of the doors. It gave way far more easily than he had expected, seeming to swing inwards under its own power. As he walked through the door memories of the vision he had experienced at Madame Voyante's barged their way uninvited to the front of his brain. He wished, for once, that he had actually paid less attention at school. Although he still had no idea what Chimera actually was, all he could think of was the goat-headed monster of myth and legend.

His previous rather fragile belief that this meeting was worth the risk was rapidly draining away and leaving in its place a persistent, nagging, scared feeling that was increasingly hard to ignore. Squaring his shoulders and trying his best to mentally squash his nerves, he stepped inside the office and was surprised to find that the room he entered was both smaller and more dimly lit than he had expected. Adam had presumed that he would be walking into a grand office similar to the others they had visited before, with long windows giving a view over the Weave, but from the murky look of the room there were no windows of any kind. The only light came from the slightly sickly glow of two of the strangely glowing lamps he had seen elsewhere in the building. The room also appeared to be very sparsely decorated, although Adam couldn't make out the walls of the office too clearly, the gloom too thick to see through. The limited light that the room did contain was focused on a small desk at its very centre, and it was this that drew Adam's attention.

Like the rest of the room, the desk was surprisingly plain and functional and the man sat waiting patiently for Adam behind the desk was also painfully average looking. He looked so very normal that Adam couldn't help but think it had to be deliberate, no one could possibly look that completely and utterly unremarkable by accident or coincidence. He was middle-aged, appearing to be neither particularly short nor tall, (or at least as far as Adam could tell, as the man remained seated). He was wearing a well-tailored, although plain, suit over a white shirt. Dark brown hair peppered with grey was slicked back from a high forehead, framing a long and finely featured face. The only thing that stood out as slightly unusual was the fact he was wearing dark brown leather gloves, hands resting on the desk in front of him, despite the warmth of the day and the slightly muggy atmosphere of the dark room. Upon seeing he had Adam's attention he leant back in his chair comfortably, seeming to be completely at ease.

"Hello Adam," he said, his voice deep and warm. "So good to finally meet you." He smiled at the confusion on Adam's face. "Not what you expected am I?"

Adam didn't know whether to nod or shake his head, "I thought that a Chimera was…"

"You thought I might be some sort of monster," the man concluded for him, looking down at himself. "Body of a lion, tail of a snake, all that mythological rubbish." He leant forward again slightly as he continued to speak, pinching the bridge of his nose and squeezing his eyes closed as if trying to dispel a persistent headache. "It's amazing how many people make that mistake… to start with. But there are other meanings for the word, do you know what they are?"

Adam shook his head, "No, but I suppose you are going to tell me."

At this the man nodded, still smiling patiently. "Of course… it's amazing what you can learn if you keep an open mind." Adam stared for a moment, convinced he had heard someone else say the same thing not too long ago, before the man continued. "Another lesser-known meaning is that a Chimera is an illusion or dream, which seems entirely appropriate considering where we are. However in this case it is the third meaning that is the important one, the one that I am sure will interest you in particular. It means a mix of two species, a being that wasn't supposed to be." He shot a penetrating look at Adam, "I think you probably know more about that than most people." His voice became more serious. "A human mother and a dream being for a father. You are very much a Chimera yourself when you think about it." He removed his fingers from the bridge of his nose and smiled again, raising his gloved hands palm forwards and open in a show of peace. "So you see, I am not the monster that you may have thought. In fact perhaps you and I are more similar than you first thought."

As he finished talking the man slowly reached across with one hand to peel back the fingers of the leather glove covering the other. Rather than the pale skin that Adam expected to see, what was revealed was a gently wavering glow in the shape of a hand. Looking more closely each of the insubstantial fingers were glimmering softly as if lit from within by a series of tiny shining stars. The sight was strangely hypnotic and Adam found it surprisingly difficult to look away from the hand and back at the man's face. "I know exactly how you feel," the man continued. "To be half of one thing and half of another. Leaves you wondering exactly where you fit into the world doesn't it?"

"No," Adam replied, with as much conviction as he could manage, despite the uncomfortable feeling of uncertainty that washed over him when Chimera spoke about their similarities. "No... I know where I fit. This world and mine, I belong in both of them and I'm happy with that."

The man behind the desk didn't react, instead he just smiled back at Adam, as if he was indulging a small child who didn't know any better, and slowly pulled the dark leather gloves back onto his hand, the glow disappearing as he did so.

"I could have... dealt with the problem you presented to me any number of times." Chimera circled his finger around, indicating the surrounding office. "The company... my company has significant resources at its disposal and I have been encouraged on several occasions to deal with you." He paused again, leaning back in his chair casually. "But you interest me Adam. Like it or not, I see many similarities between us, so I wanted to make sure you were given every chance to modify your rash behaviour. A chance to see things my way."

"Is that what Mr. Twitch and Jingle were doing?" Adam shot back at him, angry at the lack of concern on Chimera's face and even angrier at himself for the lingering doubt that was lurking somewhere in the back of his mind, a doubt fed by the secrets about his parents that others had tried to keep from him. "Were they looking out for my wellbeing when they attacked me and Nora, when they hurt my friends?"

"They were perhaps a little... overzealous," Chimera conceded. "Despite all the good that we do there are a surprising number of people who would like to see us fail. Whatever you may think, the future is coming and you, your friends, the Dreamer himself can't stop it."

Adam thought back to his vision of the Dreamer, the bead of sweat on his forehead, the feeling of sickness. "You don't understand, you're hurting people in my world too... and you're hurting the Dreamer. The whole of Reverie is in danger."

Chimera lifted his head at Adam's last comment. "I know." He smiled again, but this time the smile wasn't casual and relaxed, or friendly, or patient. It was hungry and frayed the edges. With that smile, the temporary doubt and uncertainty that had troubled Adam cleared like mist, hanging thick around him one moment and completely gone in the next. "As a result of coming into contact with the treated weave, dreamers started to react differently. Their dreams became more... malleable." Chimera's smile widened, the cultured façade flickering for a moment. The smile was still a little too manic, the eyes sparkling with previously concealed madness. "Clement was concerned, said we needed to stop the project until we had solved the side effects. He didn't understand... controlling dreamers wasn't a side effect of the project... it was the project."

Adam stared at Chimera wide-eyed as he continued. "Isenbard underestimated you and your friends. He always relied upon brute force, that ridiculous Horror that he was so proud of. But the Horror was a throwback to previous times, one big show of force, easily defeated. This is different, infinite, this is real control." Slowly rising from his seat Chimera pushed his chair back and stepped away from the desk.

"I wanted to give you a chance," he told Adam. "I thought, perhaps foolishly, that you might understand." He looked deep into Adam's eyes. "There is too much chaos in this world, especially here in Moonshine. There is an opportunity to make things better and all I need is for you and your friends to step aside."

Adam was still staring at Chimera as he spoke, horrified by what he was hearing and realising that his emotion was all too obviously reflected in his expression.

"But I don't think that you see things my way, do you Adam? I can see it all too clearly in your eyes." Chimera paused, gesturing around him, as Adam's eyes adjusted further to the darkness of the office, he realised his attention had been distracted for far too long. Gathering around the edges of the room, blinking into existence one after another, were the familiar, eerily silent, figures of infected Sleepwalkers.

"It seems that, despite a few shallow similarities you are not like me at all. You lack... vision. The Queen requires your end and there seems no further reason for me to delay that."

"The Queen?" Adam asked in confusion, "You mean Deliria?"

At this Chimera gave a short and unpleasant barking laugh. "That painted freak-show, she is no Queen. She is an evolutionary dead end, a random dream that somehow held onto some pretence of life. No, my Queen is someone... is something quite different." He shuddered slightly as he spoke and for a moment Adam was reminded, rather unpleasantly, of Isenbard and the way he had seemed to shake involuntarily when spoke of the 'help' he had received within the Horror.

Looking around him Adam could see that more of the blank-faced Sleepwalkers had now appeared within the room. Their lack of expression somehow making them appear even more intimidating.

"With you out of the way all that will remain is to deal with the puzzle that Deliria represents once and for all," Chimera said, as he made his way slowly towards the back of the room. "She seems determined to save this terrible place and despite her tainted nature, she is not without influence. Even now I can feel her, she is wrapped all around this place like an overprotective mother. I really need to find out what it is that makes her tick."

Adam could see Chimera's slim, refined features twist into a scowl as he spoke.

"What are you going to do to her?" Adam asked, but Chimera just smiled again, back to a slim-lipped and pale imitation of happiness without the genuine snarling emotion of before.

"Goodbye Adam," and with that he turned and made his way out the door at the back of the office. With a hiss of movement the door slid closed behind him, after which there was a series of further clicks and clanks which Adam suspected meant that the door was unlikely to be easy to open again.

The sound of the door closing seemed to energise the Sleepwalkers, who one after the other turned towards Adam, before shuffling slowly forward. Adam's eyes darted from left to right, trying to spot an escape route, but the office seemed to be suddenly full of the shambling figures with no clear way out. Then his heart stopped mid-beat as his eyes settled on one of the figures surrounding him. Standing there right in front of Adam, his expression as slack and lifeless as the rest of them, was Charlie.

Back-peddling away from the approaching throng Adam called across to his friend, trying to keep calm despite the panic which felt like it was trying to push its way out the front of his chest.

"Charlie... Charlie it's me, Adam. Come on mate, you know me. You know this place... we've talked about it lots of times." But his shout was just met with a blank stare as Charlie continued to lurch towards him.

Although he hadn't really expected a reaction, Adam was still disappointed. Every film he had seen when the hero's friends or family were mind controlled or brainwashed had led to him to believe that all you had to do was shout 'snap out of it', while looking pretty emotional and they would suddenly remember themselves, but it looked like that wasn't going to work here. He even tried running through a quick mental montage of happy memories he had shared with Charlie, willing Charlie to remember them too, to remember him, but that didn't work either. "Stupid lying films," Adam scowled to himself as he continued to back away from the advancing wall of Sleepwalkers.

By now Charlie and the other dreamers had almost reached him. Adam could feel the hard edge of the desk behind him and with nowhere else to go hoisted himself awkwardly onto it, scrabbling with his hands and feet to push himself away as the closest of the Sleepwalkers reached out towards him. Leaning back to avoid the grasping hands Adam lost his balance and tipped backwards off the desk, landing uncomfortably on the hard floor on the other side. The impact rattled his brain and for a moment his vision went fuzzy, only clearing as the looming face of Charlie and the mass of other dreamers appeared over him.

He felt hands grabbing loosely at him, the first few of which he was able to shake off fairly easily, their grip limp and lifeless. But as more and more of the dreamers surrounded him it became increasingly difficult, the sheer volume overwhelming him. Still shaken by his fall Adam struggled to focus his mind sufficiently to form a decent daydream. Shaking his arms loose for a moment he still managed to clap his hands together, creating a small shockwave which knocked a number of the Sleepwalkers back across the room, but they were almost immediately replaced by others and within moments Adam was again at risk of being overwhelmed.

As the gathering dreamers blocked out the last of the limited light above him, remembering Grimble's words Adam pulled the small blue cylinder from his pocket, gripping it tightly. Straining against the hands now pinning him down, he reached across and gripped the slim cord hanging from the top of the tube.

"Sorry about this Charlie," Adam muttered, and with a final effort, pulled on the cord as hard as he could.

For a moment nothing happened, the pressure of the dreamers pressing down on him becoming too much for Adam to bear. Breathing was increasingly difficult and Adam could hear the dull throbbing of his own heartbeat echoing loudly in his ears. Then there was a loud popping noise from the small tube he still held tightly and he felt it rapidly heating up in his grip. Matching the increase in heat he could feel a growing pressure from the cylinder and then, with a second louder noise, that pressure blasted out in a wave that exploded uncontrollably in all directions. Adam found himself in the centre of a raging storm that had sprung up from nowhere, tossing the dreamers that had enveloped him around the room like ragdolls. As the flying bodies hit the walls or ceiling they popped back out of existence, which Adam desperately hoped meant they had awoken safely back in the Waking World. Despite this he still winced when he saw Charlie get buffeted into the ceiling with a very painful sounding crunch, before he too blinked out of the room.

Adam's hands were aching with the effort of holding onto the cylinder, but he was far too worried about what would happen if he lost control of it to risk loosening his grip even slightly. It seemed that stood right in the eye of the sudden storm he was okay, but anywhere away from the centre looked far from safe, with the last remaining Sleepwalkers still being blasted around the room, dangling in the air like puppets whose strings had been cut. Just as the storm started to settle slightly, he was disturbed by a knock at the door and a nervous sounding voice.

"Mr. Chimera?" There was a short pause and then the voice piped up again. "Mr. Chimera, is everything alright. I heard a disturbance."

By now Adam was the only one left in the room and as the door back into the main corridor swung open he was already running, ducking under the outstretched arm of the tall Sornette woman who had pushed the door open, a look of complete bewilderment settling over her face as she looked in through the doorway. The previously ordered office was a scene of complete chaos, the desk overturned and scattered paperwork still circling like a flock of startled birds in the remnants of the localised storm that Adam had unwittingly released.

Adam took advantage of her temporary confusion to throw the tube back into the office behind him and had made it half-way down the corridor back towards the landing before he heard the first shouts of alarm. Skidding on the smooth flooring he exited the corridor, arms pin-wheeling wildly, and slid to a halt against the low wall of the first-floor stairwell, looking down over the expanse of the main atrium.

Several of the uniformed security guards were making their way up the stairs, batons gripped tightly in gloved hands. Without waiting to think too much about what he was doing Adam grabbed hold of the top of the balustrade and used it to vault straight over the side. Concentrating as hard as he could to block out all of the surrounding distractions, including the rapidly approaching and very hard looking ground, Adam squeezed his eyes closed and remembered the sensation of flight from his previous dreams. He was travelling too fast, and the distance was too short, to completely stop his fall. But it was still enough to slow him and when he hit the floor of the atrium, although it jarred his legs painfully, he was able to roll without hurting himself too badly. Lucid and the others were by his side in moments.

"What on earth happened?" Nora asked, her eyes wide. "We heard a loud bang and then you suddenly come flying out."

"It didn't go completely to plan," Adam admitted, "I think we need to leave... immediately."

The security guards on the stairway seemed torn between turning back around to follow Adam or continuing on to the first floor, where the Sornette woman was still shouting for help. Taking advantage of this temporary confusion Adam and his friends were out of the main doors and running down the road towards the edge of Moonshine before anyone at the reception thought to try and stop them leaving.

By the time they reached the edge of the city Grimble waved for them to slow down, the effort of running on his injured leg too much for him to maintain. Leaning heavily on the gaudy walking stick he still had from Deliria's palace, he managed to pant out a question. "So Adam, what happened?"

"Well I did meet Chimera," Adam said. "And Mittens was right… he wasn't quite human. But he wasn't a monster either. He seemed to be half dream being… although he wasn't happy about it." Adam spotted a meaningful glance exchanged between Lucid and Grimble as he said this.

"He is behind everything that is going on though… and he knows about the effect it is having on the Dreamer too, I think that it's all part of his plan. Clement was just a stooge, I don't think he really knew what he was getting into."

"Hmmph… not really a surprise," Grimble replied. "He was too much of a self-important stuffed shirt to be the real problem. So now what?"

Adam stopped short as he remembered the last thing that Chimera had said before left.

"Deliria!" Adam said, "Chimera is going after Deliria. We have to get to the palace as quickly as we can."

CHAPTER 18

As they approached the walls that surrounded the palace and its gardens Nora paused for a moment and signalled for the others to stop.

"More of those strange infected Sleepwalkers," she hissed. "I can feel them approaching. And there are a lot of them this time." Adam looked in the direction she was indicating and within a few moments spotted a cluster of the odd, shambling dreamers making their way towards them, emerging from one of the narrow side alleys that fed into the square in front of the palace. Then another group shuffled into view from a second alley and a third shortly after that, all seeming to be converging on the spot where Adam and his friends now stood. Nora flexed her fingers and Adam could see the darkness spilling across her eyes as she spoke. "You three go and deal with Chimera, I will stop these unfortunate dreamers from following you."

"Will you be all right?" Adam asked. "There's an awful lot of them."

"Pah!" Nora replied dismissively, but now in Mittens' familiar rougher tones. "I think I can deal with a few dreaming humans. It's what I was made to do." She gave a rather hungry smile as she spoke and Adam got the uncomfortable feeling that she was looking forward to it.

"Fine," he said. "But don't hurt them...okay."

"Alright Mr. Goody two-shoes. I'll make sure to play nicely," she told him, before turning to face the increasing mass of Sleepwalkers, cracking her small knuckles noisily as she did so.

As they walked across the grounds that led to the palace, rather than the two gaudily dressed guardsman who had previously been on duty, they were met with the unwelcome sight of Mr. Twitch lounging cat-like on the stone surround that ran alongside the steps, casually tossing and catching one of his long, slim nightmare blades. Each flick of his wrist resulted in the dark shard spinning several times in the air, glinting as the sun caught the tip or one of the dangerously sharp edges, before he would nonchalantly catch it again, looking like the world's most sociopathic juggler. He spotted them a split second after they saw him and before they got any closer, he sprang to his feet.

A few steps closer and Adam could see that their last meeting had left a few marks on Mr. Twitch, despite his apparently inhuman resilience. His sharply tailored suit was less crisp than Adam remembered, and there was a long and ugly looking rip down one of his jacket sleeves. The grim top hat, with its garland of teeth, was also looking more battered and despite the ease with which he had sprung to his feet, Adam noticed that Mr. Twitch only held a long nightmare blade in one of his hands. His other arm hung unmoving and awkward by his side.

"If he is here," Grimble growled across at Adam, "then Jingle likely won't be far away either. Keep your eyes... and your ears open boy." Adam nodded, risking a quick look around, but couldn't immediately see or hear any sign of Mr. Twitch's nasty Drömer companion. There were however far too many places around the ornamental gardens that surrounded the palace entrance where someone could easily hide themselves, so he didn't feel particularly reassured.

"Chimera thought some of you might get here sooner or later..." Mr. Twitch informed them, his foot tapping an impatient rhythm in time with his words. "...but I don't think he particularly wants to be disturbed."

"Then he will be sorely disappointed," Grimble grunted back at him, as he and Lucid split up, each one heading out to different sides, trying to make it difficult for Mr. Twitch to watch them both at the same time. Adam was left standing alone in the centre of the wide gravel pathway as the other two fanned further out. Then as he walked slowly forward, trying to keep one eye behind him in case Jingle made an appearance, Adam was disturbed by a shriek of distress from within the palace.

At the sound of the scream both Lucid and Grimble burst into a run, although in Grimble's case this was limited to a slightly awkward high speed limp. As both converged on Mr. Twitch he snarled, whipping a long nightmare blade lightning-fast towards Lucid, who only just ducked back out of the way in time. Meanwhile Grimble had also drawn close enough to attract his attention, rummaging in his pockets and pulling out another of his strange vials. Without pausing he threw it towards Mr. Twitch's head, who slashed at the flying vial with a sneer, cutting it cleanly in two as it approached him. "Pathetic," he snarled dismissively, then he paused, a disbelieving look slowly spreading across his face. Where the vial had been smashed, some of its content had splashed onto him and what had previously been a thin and colourless liquid was rapidly hardening into a gooey green gel, making it increasingly hard for him to move. Before he had the chance to react further Lucid had rushed back in towards him and swinging his long right arm, caught him a resounding crack on the chin.

The confused look still stuck on his unpleasant face, Mr. Twitch was knocked flying several metres into the undergrowth of the gardens, where he lay unmoving. Adam noticed the nightmare blade Mr. Twitch had been holding fizzling into nothingness, in moments becoming nothing more than dark smoke. Nodding to Lucid in unspoken congratulation, Grimble hobbled on towards the main doors to the palace, Adam close behind him. Lucid followed shortly after, rubbing his knuckles gingerly and still looking more than a little surprised by his success.

As soon as they entered the throne room, where they had previously met with Deliria in more comfortable circumstances, the reason for the cry was obvious. Rather than being sat in the old, comfortable armchair as she had been the last time Adam had seen her, Deliria was sat unmoving on the grand (and far less comfortable) throne. Chimera stood just to one side of her, a cruel smile on his face, while directly to either side of Deliria, holding her arms fixed tightly against the arm-rests of the throne were two, very large, Sleepwalkers.

"Hello Adam," he snarled. "I thought that the disturbance I heard must have been you or your friends. No one else would be so foolish. I had hoped that you wouldn't leave my office but it seems you are as resilient as I had been told. Perhaps I did underestimate you after all."

"Let Deliria go," Grimble growled at him.

"Not a chance," Chimera replied, with a barking laugh. "I didn't want to hurt her... or at least not straight away. I just want to find out more about her. Find out how she does... whatever it is she does to Moonshine. Find a way to replicate it, to improve it. But your arrival changes things."

Thinking back to the factory, to the Weave and the experiments that Chimera had carried out, Adam knew that they couldn't let Deliria be taken. Whatever Chimera wanted from her he would take by force, experimenting on her like a lab rat. It was a thought that made his blood boil. Adam went to take an impulsive step forward, but Lucid prevented him with an outstretched arm.

"Not now," he said to Adam, "anything could trigger him into hurting Deliria."

Realising the sense in Lucid's words Adam tried his best to calm himself, drawing a deep, slowing breath. He decided to try a different approach, a thought had been tickling the back of his mind for a while, and now seemed as good a time as any to see if he was right.

"So why did you choose here, why Moonshine?" he asked, trying to keep his voice as calm and even as possible. "You seem to like things to be organised, to be structured. This place... it's none of those things."

"Exactly," Chimera hissed back, beginning to pace back and forth as he spoke, his previously smooth and self-controlled demeanour increasingly giving way to something far more primal.

A single strand of his otherwise slick hair was hanging loosely over his eyes, and as he spoke a couple of flecks of stray spittle flew from his mouth. "If I could impose order here, of all places, where madness rules, then nothing would be beyond my reach." As he spoke his hands squeezed reflexively and Adam could see Deliria's grimace as the Sleepwalkers, seeming to react to Chimera's actions, pressed down harder on her arms. Adam looked back at her and willed her to be strong... and to understand what he was trying to get across to her.

"Okay, but I still don't understand why you hate this place so much?" Adam asked Chimera, trying to keep his tone neutral.

"Look at me," Chimera said, moving one of his gloved hands slowly to the other. Grabbing hold of the glove he pulled it clear of his hand, one finger at a time, before dropping it onto the ground, revealing the glowing mass that took the place of his hand once again.

"I never wanted this, this impurity, this mixed blood. There is a chaos in me, an unwanted gift from my parents... and I will see it gone. Here, at the centre of Moonshine, I feel it the most." He looked across at his glowing hand for a moment, wiggling the fingers in front of his eyes as if he was seeing them for the first time. His voice calmed slightly as he continued speaking, leaving him sounding almost wistful. "I will ensure that order reigns, first here... and then over all of Reverie. Science will take the place of all these foolish dreams and one day... one day I will find a way to make myself whole again. She promised me..."

"It must be hard for you to cope with being here," Adam continued, still speaking to Chimera, but looking into Deliria's eyes as he did so. "The whole place is constantly on the brink of complete chaos. It's only held in check by the presence of the Queen. That's why you couldn't afford to get rid of Deliria, no matter how much you might have wanted to. That's why, despite all your threats, you can't truly harm her now. If she was to let go of the control she exerts over Moonshine, for even a minute, the results would be unimaginable."

As he finished speaking, he saw a flicker of understanding in

Deliria's eyes and a moment later she closed her eyes tightly. As she did so the strange collection of objects which had been circling her blinked, one after another, out of existence.

"What are you doing?" Chimera shouted furiously. "Stop... I command you to stop." But there was no response, Deliria had slumped forward in the throne, only held in place by the heavy, unmoving hands of the Sleepwalkers.

Grimble cast a sideways look at Adam. "What has she done?" he muttered half under his breath.

"She has let go," Adam replied. "She's stopped doing... whatever it is she does to keep Moonshine under control."

"Oh goodness..." Grimble groaned, trying to keep panic from his voice "I'm not sure that was such a good idea Adam... I think that things are about to get really, really odd."

A couple of seconds later and Grimble's fears were realised, the first sign of the impending weirdness being several of the highly polished floor tiles leaving the ground and spinning suddenly into the air before popping like balloons, sprinkling shards of tile and a cloud of dust across the room. Adam ducked as one of the tiles exploded directly over his head, showering him with tiny sharp particles that stung the back of his hands as he held them protectively above his face. As Adam peered back out between his fingers it was clear that this was only the beginning, the tip of a very big and extremely chaotic iceberg. Not for the first time this week Adam wondered if he had, once again, gone too far... much, much too far.

The previously solid surface of the raised dais where Chimera now stood with Deliria was rippling like water, waves of movement running from one side to the other. Chimera had managed to avoid the first of the undulating stones, stepping nimbly across as the pulse of movement passed him, but the second, faster wave had caught him squarely in the legs, knocking him over. As he fell the Sleepwalkers who had been holding Deliria in place blinked out of existence. Without their restraint, she toppled forward and rolled awkwardly away from the dais, before coming to an abrupt stop a few metres from Adam and the others. Ignoring the continuing shower of dust and debris filling the air Adam ran over to her, dropping to his knees and lifting her head as gently as he was able. As he did her eyes flickered open and she managed a weak smile.

"It's alright young man... honestly. For as long as I can remember I have kept all the madness of Moonshine within me, but I get so tired... never resting for fear of what would happen... so very, very tired. If anything this is a relief."

As she finished her sentence her eyes began to close again and the chalky whiteness covering her face started to fade away, like ice slowly melting, revealing soft, pink and much healthier looking skin beneath.

"Help her!" Adam shouted across at Grimble, who nodded briefly before tossing his ridiculous walking stick to one side and lifting Deliria with surprising gentleness. Limping heavily he made his way through the increasingly chaotic throne room, down the reception corridor and towards the main entrance, never appearing to take his eyes off Deliria's unconscious face despite the dangers all around. Meanwhile, on the dais, Adam could see that Chimera was rapidly losing any last vestige of self-control, raging against the swirling madness. Lashing out wildly with his glowing hands he smashed flying tiles and blocks from the air, seeming to be completely unaware of his surroundings, his eyes glazed and staring wildly into the middle distance.

"Adam, we have to go, the palace is coming apart," Lucid shouted, pointing up at the ceiling. Looking up Adam could see a widening spider's web of cracks spreading across the ceiling.

"What is it about Moonshine and collapsing buildings," Adam groaned to himself before turning and following Lucid, who was already running in long, slightly unsteady strides towards the exit.

As they burst out of the main gates of the palace, Adam could see that the instability that had been concentrated in the throne-room was rapidly spreading. The outer walls were now flickering between various brightly coloured patterns, each more psychedelic than the last, while in the garden several of the larger trees and bushes looked like they were growing in reverse, shrinking rapidly and then vanishing into the ground with a revolting sucking noise.

Running as fast as they could manage, worried that the path under them would vanish at any moment, they made their way through the palace grounds and out of the gates.

CHAPTER 19

As Adam ran out of the palace gates, the ornate metalwork began melting into a pool of glowing liquid, droplets of the molten metal burning a series of small holes in his jeans as they splashed off the ground.

Wincing through the pain, just ahead of him Adam could see Grimble was also beginning to slow his pace, the combination of carrying Deliria and his still injured leg wearing down his natural toughness. Although Adam was tempted to offer his help somehow he knew, particularly in this case, that it would be refused, so he settled for jogging alongside his companion instead. As he drew level Grimble shot him a sideways glance.

"I told you things would get odd," he said, unable to completely hide the satisfaction in his voice, despite the dire circumstances. "That's the problem with you youngsters, no thought about the repercussions of your actions."

Adam just shrugged, or at least raised his shoulders slightly higher while still maintaining his run.

"Couldn't think of anything else," he managed to pant, "and I didn't want him to do anything to Deliria, so I had to improvise."

At the mention of Deliria's name Grimble's stern expression softened slightly.

"I'm with you there at least," he said. "Strange a place as Moonshine is, it needs Deliria…"

They stopped speaking for a moment as they ran around the corner into the next street, Adam puffing with effort and Grimble wincing as he turned rather awkwardly on his bad leg, although Lucid seems comfortable, loping along with long easy strides slightly ahead of them both. After the first few metres the street widened out into another of the informal open markets that were so popular throughout Moonshine, brightly patterned cloth canopies and hoardings spread haphazardly all the way down each side. It looked like the edge of the radiating chaos had already reached this far, with several of the canopies having taken on a life of their own, flapping like giant, horribly coloured birds. While most of the people in the street were running around in panic one trader was gamely hanging onto his stall despite it steadily rising into the air as its bright blue and yellow canopy made a determined break for the sky. Adam stepped forward to try and reach for the man's legs.

"No thank-you!" the man snapped down at him as he continued to rise into the air, "I have this completely under control, so if you could please leave me alone."

As the stall flew higher, now out of reach, Adam slowly lowered his arm and for a moment, he, Lucid and Grimble couldn't do anything other than stare as the dangling figure grew smaller and smaller, before disappearing off into the distance with a final, rather faint, cry of "I'm fine thank you very much!"

"I know this might not be the best time," Grimble said, taking advantage of the temporary pause to get the others attention, "but we need to stop, at least for a minute." He looked down pointedly at Deliria's slumped form, still cradled in his arms.

Lucid nodded, "Very well, but we can't afford to stay still for long."

A short distance away Adam spotted the doorway to one of the low stone houses hanging open, looking like it had been abandoned in a hurry, presumably when the wave of chaotic strangeness had passed through the area.

"We could try in there I suppose," he said, pointing it out to the others, "but I don't know how safe anywhere around here will be at the moment."

As if to highlight this point several large bowls that had

been stacked on the nearest traders table grew tiny clay legs and jumped down onto the ground before running off down the street in a miniature, very strange, convoy.

Without pausing to discuss things any further Grimble barged his way past the other two and through the open doorway. By the time Adam and Lucid had followed him into the cottage he had already laid Deliria down on the rickety sofa in the centre of a low ceilinged living room, before slowly collapsing onto the nearest chair with a groan, clutching his bad leg as he did so and muttering a number of rude words under his breath.

Adam walked over to the couch and looked down at Deliria's unconscious face. It was amazing how different she was without all the strangeness of Moonshine focused around her. The unnatural powder whiteness of her skin had completely vanished and her hair was now hanging loose and dark around her. Adam presumed that this was what Deliria really looked like when all the oddness was stripped away, wondering how much she must have sacrificed to look after Moonshine for so long. As he stood there he could feel Lucid moving to stand alongside him. He was holding a damp cloth he had presumably found in the cottage's small kitchen, which he dabbed gently across Deliria's forehead.

Her slack eyelids flickered at the cold touch of the cloth and then snapped open, pupils widening and darting left and right for a moment in panic as she tried to work out where she was.

"Where am I. Chimera, we can't let Chimera..."

"Chimera has gone your Majesty," Lucid told her gently. "We had to flee the palace, after you removed your protection the whole place started to come apart. The last we saw of Chimera he was still in the throne room, the building collapsing around him."

Deliria pushed herself up onto her elbows, grunting with the effort.

"Oh dear... my poor palace," she said. "I can still remember the day we built it. It was the birth of Moonshine, a new beginning." She paused for a moment, coughing uncomfortably.

While they had been talking Grimble had also hobbled across to join them, holding a slightly grubby glass filled with water. Reaching into one of his many inside pockets he withdrew a small sachet of powder which he sprinkled into the glass. "Here," he muttered, "drink this... it should help." Resting her back against one of the cushions, Deliria did as he asked, swallowing the water in two large gulps. Whatever Grimble had added to the drink seemed to work, as her eyes brightened almost immediately and when she spoke again there was a little more strength in her voice.

"So where do we go from here?" she asked, "I presume that things have been getting... a little unusual while I was unconscious?"

"That's an understatement," Grimble said with a grimace. "It's complete chaos out there."

"I need to see, we've waited here long enough" Deliria tried again to push herself up off the sofa before slumping back down with a frustrated groan. "If you don't mind?" she asked Grimble, who nodded rather hesitantly before lifting her back onto his shoulder. "Not exactly a glamorous way to travel," Deliria muttered, "but it will have to do."

"When we leave here the next thing we need to do is find somewhere safe for you to rest," Lucid told her. "You are far too weak to do anything at the moment. After that..." He paused and straightened up as a noise from outside the cottage disturbed them. There was an increasingly loud sound of raised voices and running feet and looking out of the small, low window Adam could see a mass of people all heading in one direction past the cottage.

"It looks like something big is going on," Adam said, "perhaps we better get moving again." Lucid nodded across to him, while Grimble just squared his shoulders, shifting Deliria into a more comfortable position.

"Right, let's go," said Adam and pushing open the door, led the way back onto the streets of Moonshine.

CHAPTER 20

Stepping back out of the crooked front door, the reason for the noise outside was clear. The previously empty street was full of people and almost immediately they found themselves caught up in a rushing tide of Moonshine residents, who all seemed to be running helter-skelter down the road in the direction of the docks. Initially, Adam presumed that they were all fleeing from the chaos that had begun in the palace, but then he caught sight of a familiar dark-haired figure who stepped out of the passing crush of people, catching hold of Adam's arm to steady herself.

"Hi Nora," Adam said, realising rather guiltily that he had forgotten about her for a moment in their rush to escape the palace, "what's going on?"

"Your friend Chimera has been busy," she panted. "There are a lot... and I mean an awful lot of those weird Sleepwalkers just behind us. I don't know what you have been up to, but a few minutes ago hundreds of them started appearing all across Moonshine... and they're all headed this way!"

The exodus towards the docks made more sense to Adam now. Looking past the mass of fleeing people, some determinedly carrying as much of their makeshift homes as they could manage despite the panic, he could see a solid wall of the infected dreamers walking slowly, but inexorably, behind them. Although they were still some distance away, he was also pretty sure he could pick out the unwelcome twin figures of Mr. Twitch and Jingle.

"I really hoped we had seen the last of those two," he muttered, before turning and following Nora and the others through the crowded streets.

Caught up in the middle of the crowd it was impossible to do anything other than let the tide of people carry them along and within a few minutes they were at the ramshackle docks. The pavement below their feet gave way to wooden planks, flexing under the weight of the Moonshiners now gathering there.

As they reached the far end of the wooden walkway Grimble lowered Deliria onto the ground, leaning her as gently as he could against one of the posts that lined the docks. "Adam," he said, pointing back to the palace, which was now under a raging cloud of spinning debris. "Unless something is done soon the whole of Moonshine will descend into chaos. Stopping Chimera or those dreamers won't mean anything if the whole place tears itself to pieces."

"I know," Adam sighed. "But I don't think I can do anything, I don't know how. Only Deliria knows how to do... whatever it is she does."

"Sadly that is true," came a weak voice from behind them. Deliria had managed to push herself up so that she was now uncomfortably hunched in a half-seated position against the rough wood of the mooring post. "I wish it wasn't, you have no idea how wonderful it felt to suddenly be free of all of that, to no longer feel the pressure of Moonshine weighing down on me."

As she spoke Adam could see her look slowly around the docks, at the congregated residents of Moonshine stood staring in disbelieving horror at what was happening to their homes. Amongst the huddled clusters of desperate and hopeless looking people Adam spotted a few recognisable faces. To his left, visibly shaking, although Adam couldn't tell if it was due to cold or fear, stood their landlady. Her extravagant hairstyle had collapsed completely, her carefully hoarded money stuffed in a bag hanging loosely by her side no help to her now. A few metres further down the boardwalk the Sornette Dockmaster stood twisting his horrible oilskin top-hat between nervous fingers as he stared at the approaching collapse of the city.

Deliria saw all of this and then looked across at Adam with

an expression so sad that he could feel his insides hurting, just from the pain of looking at her.

"Oh well," she continued, seeming to be speaking more to herself than anyone else, "I suppose I can't spend all day just lying around."

She tried to push herself up onto her feet, but couldn't quite manage, the effort still too much for her. With a grimace she asked, "Seeing as none of my brave and loyal staff seem to be on hand at the moment would one of you gentlemen be so kind as to help her Royal Majesty to her feet?"

Adam started to step forward, then realised that he had been beaten to it by a slightly sheepish looking Grimble.

"Here… take my hand…" Grimble said, holding out his arm to her. A look of pleased surprise passed briefly over Deliria's face, washing away the previous sadness. Then she slowly and rather awkwardly pushed herself up onto her feet, using Grimble's outstretched arm, and eventually shoulder, to stand upright.

As she reached her feet there was a loud cracking sound in the distance as a huge chunk of masonry fell from the palace walls, hung impossibly un-moving halfway to the ground for a moment and then disappeared, sucked back into the hole it had left behind, like a huge bubble going down a plughole, stretching slightly before vanishing completely.

"Okay," taking a deep breath Deliria closed her eyes tightly and held her hands clasped in front of her, knuckles white. For a moment that seemed to stretch on infinitely the air around her head flickered uncertainly, then with a series of gentle popping noises several mismatched items blinked into existence around her, starting a slow and lazy orbit. As they appeared the soft pinkness which had briefly been visible on Deliria's cheeks began to fade away, gradually settling back into the more familiar powder white, spreading across her skin like frost on a window. Her long dark hair, already turning back to its unnaturally white blond, coiled back around into its previous swirl. It quickly gathered itself on the top of her head, moving with a life of its own and as it did so the youthful brightness in her eyes dimmed slightly. Within a few moments there was no remnant of the younger and more carefree woman that had briefly accompanied them, instead she was replaced once again by the painted, slightly doll-like figure surrounded by orbiting oddness that Adam recognised from their very first meeting.

As her transformation ended Adam could see the surrounding chaos begin to slow almost immediately, a calming wave centred on Deliria's small figure washing outwards. While the damage that had already taken place wasn't reversed, the flying chunks of masonry dropped to the ground and lay there unmoving. Around them he could hear a growing mutter of relief from the huddled residents of the city, which grew and grew in volume until one of the voices cheered Deliria, a call which jumped from mouth to mouth until the whole dock was filled with cries of celebration.

Then, just as quickly, the cheers quietened, replaced by murmurs of dismay as two figures stepped onto the far end of the boardwalk, one tall and one short, both dark-suited and dismal looking. Just behind them the massed ranks of the infected Sleepwalkers slowly advanced, spilling out onto the far end of the docks and Adam realised that, with their backs to the edge of the Weave, there was nowhere left to run.

To his surprise, rather than feeling afraid, as he had for most of his time in Moonshine, Adam realised that more than anything he felt angry. The part of his brain that always kept going off on wild tangents, even when he had much more important things to deal with, wondered briefly if perhaps he had just been through so many scary things since arriving in Moonshine, escaped so many collapsing buildings, fought off so many challenges that he had simply used up his entire 'being scared allowance' for the next hundred years. But whatever the reason he was definitely feeling angry. Angry at the way that people were being used, all the innocent dreamers unaware of the harm they were doing to Reverie. All the people who were increasingly ill back home in the Waking World. He felt angry for Deliria and all the other oddballs that made Moonshine the very strange, sometimes disturbing, but always interesting, place that it was. Angry that Chimera somehow felt that Moonshine and its inhabitants needed to be made more 'normal'. But most of all he felt angry that here and now, despite Deliria's self-sacrifice to save her people and city, that things still weren't over.

"Uh-oh," Adam heard Grimble murmur, although the sound was slightly muffled, through ears that were now throbbing in time with his increasingly rapid heartbeat. "I know that look."

Adam turned to see Grimble pretending he hadn't just been slowly backing away from him.

"Tell everyone to grab hold of something," Adam told him, trying hard to speak calmly, to do his best to dampen down the growing heat emanating from the pendant hanging around his neck.

"What was that?" Lucid asked from his other side, sounding confused. "Did you just say something?"

"Yes," Adam replied, almost shouting this time. "Tell everyone... and I mean everyone to grab hold of something right now!"

Lucid looked as if he was about to ask another question, then thinking better of it turned to the nearest Moonshiner instead and shouted for them to do what Adam had asked. Within a few moments the message was running up and down the crowds gathered on the docks. Those nearest to posts or mooring ropes grabbed hold as tightly as they could, reaching out to link arms with those who couldn't reach anything more substantial. Sornette, Drömer and humans all interlinked in one long scruffy chain. Just before he turned his attention back to the advancing Sleepwalkers Adam noticed that Grimble was gripping Deliria's hand with a particularly determined expression on his face, and even in the extremity of their current position, had to fight down a smile. Then the moment passed and he focused back on the job at hand.

He hadn't really been thinking when he had told everyone to grab hold of something, he had just known that was what they needed to do. He remembered the times he had used his daydreaming close to the Weave, how it had saved them from the approaching Horror in the past and how it had reacted to him in the Chimera factory. More than that he remembered the figure of his mother rising from the mist of the Weave and the momentary touch of her hand on his, no matter how brief and unreal it had been. He could feel the Weave behind him and realised that some of the anger he was feeling was coming from it, remembering that what Chimera had done had hurt and corrupted the Weave more than anything else.

Closing his eyes and concentrating he could feel the energy of it churning through the air around him and stretching out his arms wide to either side, he gathered as much of that energy as he could. In his mind he pictured grabbing hold of it tightly in each hand, then slowly he raised both hands into the air, hearing a collective gasp from around him as he did so. When he opened his eyes again the first thing he saw was Lucid staring across at him, a look of almost comical shock on his face. The second thing he saw was a solid wall of the mist that formed the Weave rising up above either side of the Docks, hundreds of metres high, looming over them all. Looking up at this teetering mass of mist the few gathered Moonshiners who hadn't yet grabbed hold of something or someone, did so very, very quickly. By this point the approaching Sleepwalkers had nearly reached them and right at the front of them all Adam could see Mr. Twitch and Jingle, for the first time looking unsure of themselves. Mr. Twitch had pulled yet another long nightmare blade from somewhere and Jingle still held his bell covered club, but both weapons looked insignificant to Adam now, nothing more than shiny toys when balanced against the looming mass of the Weave.

The weight of it all was becoming too much for Adam to hold, so without waiting any longer he brought both of his hands crashing down in front of him. As he did the towering wall of mist collapsed flooding across the docks like a tidal wave. There were cries and shouts from the residents of Moonshine as the wave washed over them, but Adam's warning had been taken seriously and as the wave passed he could see them still grimly hanging on to the docks or each other. Mr. Twitch and Jingle weren't so fortunate, stood in the centre of the board-walk, and the full force of the wave swept them up and away in moments, before continuing on and flooding across the horde of Sleepwalkers. As the Weave touched them each dreamer faded and then vanished completely, although he couldn't really tell from this distance, Adam thought that he saw the expressions of the dreamers regaining some awareness in the split second before they disappeared.

Then almost as quickly as it had appeared the wave was gone, flowing back across the docks and re-joining the main flow of the Weave. All around him Adam could see the people of Moon-shine. Many were blinking or staring around in confusion, some had slumped to the ground in exhausted relief and others were still determinedly hanging onto whatever post or rope had saved them, but without exception they all looked grateful to still be alive. Of Mr. Twitch and Jingle there was no sign, but in the centre of the boardwalk stood a grim looking top hat slowly spinning on its brim and directly next to it lay a small wooden club covered in bells, a couple of which had come loose and which rolled across the uneven planks of the dock, gently chiming.

CHAPTER 21

The next few days passed quickly. Adam spent his days at school or home, keeping a relieved eye on Charlie's slow but continuous recovery. After the first couple of days Charlie had been well enough to get out of bed and shortly after that he had recovered enough to eat with the rest of the family. Sat at the table in the kitchen watching Charlie crunching his way through his third bowl of pre-breakfast cereal Adam felt a wave of contentment, the warm glow of a job well done. It was still early in the morning and Mr. and Mrs. Henson weren't downstairs yet, so Adam and Charlie were able to speak freely, with Adam filling in the gaps between Charlie's crunches with the story of what had taken place in Reverie. He had decided to leave out a few details, in particular skirting around the time that Charlie had attacked him in Chimera's office, but covered the rest of the adventure as well as he could.

"So Nora's some kind of superhero now then?" Charlie asked him.

"No... not exactly," Adam replied hesitantly. "More like a supervillain that happens to be on our side at the moment. But we definitely couldn't have done it without her."

Charlie nodded and then winced, rubbing the back of his neck gingerly.

"Ouch," he grimaced. "It's weird but at the same time as I started feeling better I got this really bad ache in my back and neck, like I'd been hit really hard... which is ridiculous as I haven't got out of bed for days."

Adam looked down guiltily, concentrating on his breakfast cereal, remembering the crunch when Charlie had hit the ceiling back in Reverie, but fortunately Charlie didn't seem to notice, instead heading across the kitchen and putting a couple of slices of bread into the toaster.

Charlie wasn't the only one making a recovery, each day more and more students had been returning to Miss Grudge's class and the news reports that had warned of a countrywide epidemic were soon replaced with short, and far less hysterical, pieces on the sudden end of the illness.

Adam's nights, as always, were spent in Reverie. It had been several days since the attack at the docks and since then Moonshine had been doing what Moonshine did best... building. When Adam returned there again that night the place was already starting to look like its old self. On Deliria's orders the first point of business had been the complete demolition of the Chimera offices and factory. It had turned out that the residents of Moonshine were nearly as good as pulling buildings down as they were at putting them up. Now all that was left of the building was a pile of rubble, which was rapidly shrinking as people helped themselves to bits and pieces to use in their own rebuilding work.

Deliria had set up a makeshift throne room in the wreckage of the palace, which was slowly being rebuilt around her, but this time the dais had the comfortable armchair at its centre, Deliria having been quite insistent that the grand and very uncomfortable throne was far too badly damaged to be repaired. When Adam arrived the others were already there, and although he didn't say anything, he suspected that Grimble in particular had hardly left Deliria's side since the adventures at the docks. Deliria raised a hand in greeting.

"Greetings Adam."

"Hello your majesty, any news?" he asked.

"No, or at least nothing new," she admitted. "There is no sign of Chimera, nor of his unpleasant henchmen, although that's no bad thing. I very much hope that we've seen the last of them."

Adam nodded in agreement, if he never saw Mr. Twitch and Jingle again it would still be much too soon. It was, for example, going to be quite a while before he stopped flinching at the sound of ringing bells, which had already caused a couple of embarrassing moments back home.

"The odd Sleepwalkers have also vanished along with Chimera, including those that had been gathering around the Stairway."

Adam nodded, relieved to hear that the Stairway was once again safe. Still, despite this reassurance he knew, deep down, that it was unlikely that this would be the last time the Stairway, and the Dreamer himself, were threatened. It was altogether too much of a coincidence that both Chimera and Isenbard before him had attacked the Stairway in one form or another. Chimera's reference to his 'Queen' also sat uncomfortably at the back of Adam's head, carrying with it the feeling of a larger threat, still unresolved, something or someone that was behind both the previous appearance of the Horror and the most recent problems in Moonshine.

Still for the moment the immediate danger posed by Chimera and his scheming was gone and there were now more immediate issues to address, so rather than talking around these darker matters, Adam contended himself with more idle chatter with the three sat around the table.

Once these initial pleasantries were over Lucid, Grimble and Deliria settled back onto their previous topic of conversation, which seemed to be focused around setting up a new trade route between Moonshine and Nocturne. Adam got the impression that this route was going to be served the traditional way, using the Sornette's network of barges, with Lucid looking particularly animated and pleased with himself. Nora was stood just to one side of the group, not really involved in the discussion and looking a little more downcast than normal. As the others rejoined their conversation she waved across to Adam, pointing to the doors leading out onto the balconies overlooking the palace gardens. Adam raised his eyebrow questioningly, but the others seemed to be completely engrossed in their conversation and he didn't think he had much to add to trade discussions, so he headed across to the doors as Nora had asked.

Walking out onto the balcony, one of the few original parts of the building that had survived the traumas of the previous week relatively unscathed, Adam was treated to a panoramic view of Moonshine. He could clearly see the smouldering pile that used to be the Chimera offices off in the distance, while closer to the palace the city appeared to be thriving, new additions filling in the gaps caused by the previous chaos. As he leant forward against the balcony railings, taking a moment to admire the speed with which Moonshine was becoming whole again, Nora joined him.

"I needed to talk to you," Nora said, "and just you for the moment."

"Why, what is it?" Adam asked.

Nora looked unusually distracted and for the first time in a long while seemed unable to meet Adam's gaze.

"To be specific Mittens needs to speak to you. There is something we have been thinking about for the last couple of days and we have come to a decision." Adam turned away from the balcony to face Nora, who had started walking nervously up and down behind him.

Nora stopped her pacing, although still with her back to Adam.

"I realise now that I have to stay here," she said, although the layers in her voice made it clear that it was Mittens who was currently speaking. "I'm needed... which is an unusual feeling, but one which I think I could get used to." She turned around to face Adam as she spoke, and he could see she was smiling, although there was a hint of sadness on the edge of her expression. "So I think this is where we will have to part ways. Nora and I have already discussed and agreed what must happen, but we wanted to wait for you. It seemed only fair to say goodbye after everything we have been through together."

As she finished her sentence the oily blackness in her eyes gathered, intensified and then began to stream away from her, soon joined by matching tendrils from the friendship bracket around her wrist, which shrunk and then vanished as the swirling darkness gathered several metres away, slowly forming a figure matching Nora's.

Nora shook her head slightly, rubbing her forehead.

"Ok... that felt weird," she said, before looking up at the shimmering figure now facing them both.

"It feels strange to be myself, back in the world again," said Mittens, looking down at her hands as if seeing them for the first time. "I have spent so long travelling with you that I almost forgot what it feels like."

Adam looked across at her. She was an exact replica of Nora, although a Nora who was made entirely of a dark, shiny liquid that rippled slightly as she moved. "So is that what you look like?" Adam asked.

Mittens laughed, a slightly unpleasant bubbling sound.

"Oh no, not at all, but what I really look like would probably give you bad dreams for a year, so I thought this might be a bit more... acceptable." She turned to face Nora. "I wanted to thank you. I know it can't have been easy looking after me for so long. You're very brave... and stronger than you give yourself credit for."

Nora smiled. "You weren't such a bad guest..." She paused, her brow furrowing as a new thought occurred to her. "What will it mean for me though, with you gone will I still be able to come here, to Reverie?" Mittens looked down for a moment, appearing to concentrate. "I'm not completely sure. Your experiences have changed you, of that I am certain." She reached out her hand and Nora tentatively did the same, their fingertips touching.

Mittens smiled. "Some doors, once they are opened, are hard to close again." Then she turned to Adam. "There is something I need to tell you too," she said. "Since I have been back in Reverie I have felt something, something that I am increasingly sure of." Adam's breath caught in his throat at her next sentence. "I believe that I may know where your mother is. The longer I have been back here, the stronger my connection to the other Nightmares becomes and the more I am aware of their thoughts. I think that she is somewhere close to the place where the Nightmares come from... where I come from."

"Where, where is that?" Adam said, every sense in his body suddenly tingling, his head spinning at her words, glad that the solid stone balcony was there behind him, holding him up. "If you know where my Mum is you must tell me... please."

Mittens smiled her familiar toothy smile. "You don't need me to tell you where the Nightmares come from. Lucid, Grimble, they all know, it's just that no one... and I really mean no one, would choose to ever go there."

She raised her hand to them both. "Anyway... I really can't be doing with long, emotional goodbyes... so see you around," she said and with that the liquid form lost its shape and substance, splashing down into a dark, oily puddle. A few seconds later and the puddle had also gone, shrinking down to a pinprick and then vanishing completely. There was a brief gentle gust of wind, where Adam could have sworn he heard her voice one last time, whispering "... and it seems that Mittens is the name for a small furry pet... very amusing." Then nothing.

Adam and Nora were still stood on the balcony over an hour later when Grimble and Lucid joined them, their discussions with Deliria concluded. "Have we missed something?" Lucid asked, seeing the expression on Adam and Nora's faces.

"Mittens has gone," Nora told them, her voice quiet.

"Gone... what do you mean... gone where?" said Grimble, looking around as if he was still trying to somehow spot her somewhere on the balcony.

"We'll explain later," Adam told them, "but for the moment there is something else important that I need to ask you."

Lucid raised his eyebrow. "Go ahead."

"I think I know where my mum could be," Adam said. "It's the last thing Mittens told us before she left. She said my mum was where the Nightmares come from... and that you would know where that is."

Grimble and Lucid exchanged a quick glance and then Lucid

nodded, seemingly having reached some unspoken agreement. "This is not the only continent of Reverie," Grimble explained. "There is another, located far across the Dwam, the great sea of dreams." As Grimble spoke Adam thought back to the portrait on Bombast's wall and his tales of adventures. "And there, on the other side of the world, is the place where the Nightmares come from."

Stood high on the balcony, Adam peered under the shade of his hand, trying to see as far into the horizon as possible. "So that's where I have to go then?" he asked, disappointed that he couldn't really see anything other than the chaotic expanse of Moonshine and the flow of the Weave disappearing off into the horizon. "All the way to the other side of the world... that's where the Nightmares live... and that's where I'll find my Mum."

"So it seems," Lucid replied, "It is not an easy journey, nor is it a safe one." He smiled grimly, "so I suppose you had better not go alone."

Grimble sighed deeply as he also leant forward onto the railings, joining the others staring out into the distance. "If there is one thing that I hate even more than a river made of dreams, it's a whole ocean. Still without me I doubt either of you idiots would get very far."

Finally Nora spoke, "Don't think that you're going without me either." She grimaced slightly. "Without Mittens I'm not sure what help I will be, or even if I can reach Reverie again, but I have this strange feeling that there is something I still need to do here... and this might be it."

Adam didn't really know what to say, too full of gratitude to find the right words. Instead he settled for a smile that he hoped conveyed everything he felt.

As the sun slowly made its way out of view, dropping out of sight below the horizon, behind the bustle of Moonshine and its strange and wonderful inhabitants, the four companions stood side by side and waited for the night to fall. Waited to sleep and to wake and to dream again.

A SHORT WORD
FROM THE AUTHOR

I hope you have enjoyed the world of Reverie and Adam's continuing adventures. If you did it would be great if you could take two minutes to leave a quick review.

If you want to keep up with the latest in Reverie you can follow 'The Daydreamer Chronicles' on Facebook, you can also find the occasional update on the series website: www.daydreamerchronicles.com

Adam's adventures in Reverie will continue in the third book in the Daydreamer Chronicles: 'Where Dreams End'. Read on for a taster from the next book in the series:

WHERE DREAMS END: PROLOGUE

Isabella Farthing was bored. Really, truly, deeply and mind-numbingly bored. For someone used to a life of adventure, where taking impossible risks, facing terrible storms or over-coming dastardly enemies had become an almost unnoticed part of her daily routine, the last few days had been almost un-bearably bland. She had tried to spice up her evening the night before by picking a fight with a group of tough looking Drömer, but to her disappointment they had dealt with her deliberately rude comments with perfect manners, doing nothing more than giving her a couple of rather hurt looks before eventually leaving the inn's small and crowded bar, their drinks unfinished.

She knew that she really ought to feel guilty, but other than a lingering feeling of tiredness, she didn't really feel much at all. "Still," she reasoned to herself as she clicked her right arm into place, pulling the sleeve of her jacket down as far as she was able, with just the slightly dull brass fingers of her hand showing be-neath the cuff, "despite last night's shortcomings perhaps today would be the day that would bring something more interesting, a proper reason to get out of bed."

In truth, she doubted that today would actually offer any-thing better than any of the repetitively dull and frustrating days from the last week, but there was no harm in hoping. If nothing else there might at least be a chance of better news, some progress made on the repairs to her ship. She rolled her shoulder a couple of times to confirm that her arm was locked securely in place and then shuffled herself around on the thin mattress. Pushing herself forward, she lowered the socket strapped to her left leg onto the smooth brass peg-leg that sat ready and waiting for her at the side of the bed. Then, with a well-practiced twisting motion, she attached it and levered herself onto her feet in a single smooth movement, pausing briefly to steady herself.

Making her way to the other end of the room, which was a matter of no more than five short steps, her room being as small as it was unpleasant, she leant for a moment with her hands resting on the small cracked sink and looked at herself in the mirror. The face within the frame was still familiar, but she increasingly struggled to think of it as her own. She was certain that she must be both younger and happier than the rather tired, middle-aged woman looking back at her from within the cracked, murky glass. With a sigh, she rooted around in the bowl that sat carefully balanced on the shelf directly below the sink, eventually pulling out the small round orb that it contained, despite its best efforts to slip through her fingers which were still clumsy with early morning cobwebs.

Wincing slightly, as she did every time that she pressed the orb into the empty socket that used to hold her left eye, she blinked a couple of times and looked at herself in the mirror again. "Better," she thought, "definitely better." The piercing green of the glass eyeball, whilst in no way a match for the natural hazel of her remaining eye, was a familiar sight and one that made her immediately feel far more like herself.

Her morning routines complete, Isabella clanked and clicked her way back across to the room's door, ducking a little to fit her tall frame through the doorway. Navigating the steep, winding stairway was a tortuous affair, as it was every day, but the small attic room was the cheapest that the inn had to offer, and she needed to save every thread she could. Every morning when she made her way to the docks it seemed that it was to be informed of ever-increasing repair costs, to the point at which she was beginning to worry that she was going to be land-locked forever. A thought that she couldn't bear to contemplate for more than a moment. As Isabella left the Inn the Innkeeper scowled nervously at her, presumably due to her bad behavior the previous evening. Despite this, as she left the building the morning light was a welcome change from the dank darkness of her room, and momentarily lifted her mood.

In fact, the day proved to be extraordinarily hot, and by the time she reached the docks the brass of her right hand was glowing slightly, drawing even more curious looks than she usually got. Flimsy Jim was waiting for her when she arrived at the yard, pacing nervously up and down, muttering to himself.

"Um...h..hello B..Bella," he stuttered in greeting, looking up for a moment, before dropping his gaze and resuming his pacing.

"Morning Jim, how's my girl doing?" He grimaced at her question, and if anything, the speed of his pacing increased. As Jim had repeatedly informed her despite her complete disinterest, he suffered terribly with his nerves, with both his stutter and his pacing triggered by anxiety. From the look of him this morning he was feeling extremely nervous.

"So?" she asked again, "how are we doing?"

"Uhhm... n...not all th...that good," he managed. "The d... damage to the h...hull was w...w...w...worse than I thought."

Isabella sighed inwardly, trying to keep her temper in check. "How much worse... or more specifically, how much more expensive are we talking?" This conversation was an unpleasantly familiar one, to the point that it had pretty much become part of her daily routine. As a result, Isabella could pretty much predict what the next minute would consist of, unconsciously counting it all out in her head as she watched Jim:

1.   10 seconds of further nervous pacing
2.   A sigh as he pulled a piece of paper from the pocket of his overalls
3.   10 more seconds as he studied the paper before scrunching it back up and placing it back in his pocket. (She had never seen what was written on the paper and was increasingly convinced that there was nothing on it)

4.   Another sigh, a shake of his head and then....

"300 threads," he said. "Taking materials and labour into account it would cost another 300 threads."

Isabella felt her heart constrict at his words. After the disappointment of the last few days she thought she had become pretty used to receiving bad news, but there was no way she could find that much, not after all the costs she had already incurred. She also noticed, as she did every day, that Jim's stutter seemed remarkably absent when he was talking about money. Without realising how she had got there she found herself face to face with Jim, the material of his overalls bunched tightly in the grip of her metal hand, holding him with his feet dangling several feet off the ground.

"You little scam artist," she growled, red mist washing in from the edge of her vision. "I've had enough of your games."

"No, no, no, it's not like that at all... honestly it's not," Jim squeaked, his legs pedaling uselessly in the air and his hands grasping the solid brass knuckles still holding him aloft. "It's the m...ma...materials you need. You need the very best materials to s...su...survive on the Dwam and the best doesn't come cheap." His eyes widened as Isabella thrust her face close to his.

"I don't have that sort of money," she hissed. "You have already taken nearly everything I have."

"I can ma...maybe manage for 250..." he flinched as Isabella lifted him even higher. "O...okay... 200 threads, but that's the very b...best I can do."

Although Isabella gave him the most menacing glare she was capable of, (which she knew from experience to be pretty intimidating, the empty glow of her glass eye having broken the spirit of many an unlucky soul), it seemed that Flimsy Jim was unwilling to compromise any further, his natural greed slightly outweighing his equally natural cowardice. Despite his precarious dangling, Jim had managed to cross his arms and now just hung there, scowling.

Reluctantly she dropped him to the ground, and ignoring the stream of complaints that followed immediately after, stalked off with her brass hand clenching and unclenching in a constant, angry, cycle. More than anything she wanted to hit something, but the tiny remaining rational part of her brain knew that wouldn't help, other than to make her temporarily feel better. What she really needed was money, a lot of money, at short notice and with no real means of raising any.

As she continued to walk away from the docks her hunched shoulders slowly relaxed and then slumped as the grimness of her situation fully sank in. More than money, she knew deep down that what she really needed was a miracle.

WHERE DREAMS END: CHAPTER 1

"What we need is a miracle," Adam sighed to Grimble as they sat either side of the long ornate table which still served as the centerpiece to the old mansion's dining room. He sunk his chin into his hands despondently. "I thought you said that everyone knew where the Nightmares come from."

He was feeling thoroughly fed up and it was difficult not to let his frustrations spill out, even though he knew his friends were only trying to help. When he had found out his mother was still somewhere in the dream world, and more than that, where she was likely to be, he had been filled with almost unbearable excitement, believing for the first time in what felt like a very long while that he was going to be able to find her. He had been told that she was on the other side of Reverie, in a distant continent across the Dwam, the great sea of dreams, somewhere where the Nightmares that stalked the world came from. But that had been weeks ago, and despite their best efforts, Adam and his odd companions had failed to make any progress.

"That's true," Grimble replied, pulling Adam's attention back to the conversation at hand. "I know, Lucid knows, we all know... but getting there is not so easy."

Lucid nodded in agreement, pushing his chair back away from the table and stretching out his long limbs with a yawn. "The problem is finding a ship that is capable of crossing the Dwam, and more tricky than that, finding a captain that is willing to make the journey." He cracked his knuckles as he finished speaking, a nervous habit which Adam had noticed Lucid had picked up recently and which was emphasised by his unusually long fingers. Adam winced at the sound, rubbing at his own knuckles in sympathy.

"So, what do we do then?"

"Well," Lucid replied, "I have tried pretty much everywhere… and spoken to everyone I can think of in Nocturne…" he paused awkwardly and Adam knew what was coming next. "…everyone except Bombast."

Adam thought back to the last time they had sat together in Bombast's opulent offices at the Grand Library in the centre of Nocturne. Although it had taken a while, he had learned to see through the larger than life pantomime that Bombast portrayed to the rest of the world, past the ridiculous outfits and booming voice. He had glimpsed the shrewd, calculating brain that sat backstage in Bombasts head, hidden away but always working, pulling the levers of Nocturne and beyond. He wasn't sure if there was such a thing as a spymaster in Reverie, but if there was then Bombast was most definitely it.

He knew everything and everyone in the dream world, and so normally he would have been the first person that they would have gone to for advice or help, especially as, according to Bombast, he had attempted to sail the Dwam himself in his wilder youth. But their relationship with Bombast had been damaged, perhaps irreparably, by the events that had recently taken place in the distant and very unusual city of Moonshine. While they had managed to save the city and deal with the terrible threat it had faced, this had also resulted in the disappearance of Bombast's brother into the mists of the Weave. Although it hadn't been Adam's fault, instead being the result of a clash with some of the other, highly unpleasant, employees of Chimera, he had been present when Bombast's brother had tumbled into the pink mists. Adam also knew that the only reason the clash had taken place was because of him, and so he still felt responsible. It was an unpleasant feeling that had rested on his shoulders ever since, like a damp, heavy, miserable scarf.

He had gone to visit Bombast, accompanied by Lucid, as

soon as they had returned, but Bombast had refused to see them, too consumed by grief at the disappearance of his brother. Lucid had tried several times since then to meet with his old friend... to get the chance to explain what had happened back in Moonshine, but so far without any success. Despite all of this Adam was pretty sure that even now, if Bombast was made aware of the desperate nature of their need, he would somehow see his way to helping them, but he was similarly sure that if there was any way to solve their current predicament without troubling Bombast again then they should take it. The only true solution was to give Bombast time and space, letting his oversized heart recover from its pain, then they could talk, and eventually try and rebuild their friendship.

"It's fine," Adam told him. "I really want to talk to Bombast too, but it's still too soon. We'll have to think of something else."

Grimble leant forward across the table, his heavy-set face resting on steepled fingers. He looked exhausted, the scars on his face seeming more pronounced than normal, the grey of his hair more noticeable. "There is someone else," he said, his deep, gravelly voice sounding as tired as he looked. He turned to look at Lucid. "You could ask Granny."

"Granny?" repeated Adam incredulously, trying without complete success to stifle a laugh. "Who's Granny?"

Lucid looked back across at him grimly. "Not someone you laugh at for a start," he replied, "and not someone that I would choose to speak to... and definitely not to ask for help."

He sighed quietly to himself before continuing, "but Grimble is right, I can't think of anything... or anyone else, no matter how bad an idea it might end up being."

"So, you will go and see her then?" Grimble asked.

"Yes... if I must, I will take Adam with me, but you can stay here," Lucid told him. "My nerves can't take having you two in the same room again. Last time we were lucky to get out in one piece."

"She just needs to learn how to accept a bit of constructive criticism," Grimble harrumphed, although he didn't argue. Instead, he slumped a little lower in his seat, giving off waves of silent disapproval.

"Come on then." Lucid tapped Adam on the shoulder before leading the way out of the Mansion and back into the streets of Nocturne.

The first part of their journey was familiar to Adam, the route down to the docks dotted with the normal mixture of daily traffic, bustling street traders and the occasional wandering dreamer. Stepping aside to let a small girl run past, closely pursued by her Nightmare, (which for some reason on this occasion was an angry looking monkey on a tricycle), Adam asked again exactly where they were headed.

"Today we will be going a little further into the docks than you have been before," Lucid told him. "Until now you have seen... perhaps the better side of the city. But as with most places, there are parts of Nocturne which are less pleasant, and that is where we will find Granny."

Whether it was the effect of Lucid's words or something more palpable, Adam was sure he could feel a change in atmosphere as they passed the more familiar sights, sounds and smells of the dockside bazaar and entered an area he didn't recognize. Following closely behind Lucid, he weaved his way between a series of brick buildings and run-down wooden warehouses, all looming mournfully above them.

It didn't take long for Adam to completely lose his sense of direction as they made their way through the maze of rotten buildings, although Lucid continued to stride confidently ahead, with Adam lagging a few metres behind.

Lucid temporarily disappeared from sight as he walked around a corner just ahead, their route squeezing uncomfortably between several particularly tall pitted brick buildings. As Adam followed him around the corner he stopped short, startled by the odd sight now directly in front of him. Lucid was stood facing the biggest man that Adam had ever seen. Despite Lucid's height, the man stood taller than Lucid and his top hat combined… and was at least five times wider. Gulping to himself Adam walked up to join them.

The hulking figure bent down slightly, bringing its huge face level with Lucid's, although still towering above Adam. "Ullo Mr. Lucid," it rumbled, the voice so deep that Adam swore he could feel it vibrating up through his feet.

"Hello Carter," Lucid replied, smiling up at the massive man currently blocking their way. "How are things with you?"

"Can't complain, Mr. Lucid, Granny keeps me busy."

"And have you been behaving yourself, Carter?" Lucid asked, seeming to be completely at ease despite the less than pleasant surroundings and the fact that the hulking figure he was chatting with had fists much bigger than his head.

"Heh, depends on your definition I s'pose Mr. Lucid. I do what Granny says to do… so you'd best ask her."

Straightening up, Carter stepped slightly to one side, leaving a small gap between him and the nearest wall. One massive hand gestured towards the doorway behind him.

"Through you go then… make sure you behave though Mr. Lucid. I wouldn't want to have to 'urt you," he added as they walked past, Adam pressing himself closer to the wall than he probably needed to, scraping his back against the rough brickwork.

As they entered the doorway the gloom of the alleyway deepened even further, Adam's eyes slowly catching up with rest of his body and adjusting to the darkness.

"Who was that?" Adam asked as they made their way down a dark and rather musty corridor, the walls of which were paneled in a rich dark wood that seemed out of keeping with the otherwise grubby surroundings.

"Carter?" Lucid replied, running his fingers nonchalantly along the paneling. "I've known him since he was little, or at least littler than he is now. He's not a bad fellow at heart, but he is unfortunately rather easily influenced… and for the last few years Granny has been the one doing the influencing." He stopped, flicking the gathered dust from his fingers with a tutting sound. "Sadly, Granny is not the best role model, but she looks after him and keeps him out of trouble… other than the trouble she wants of course."

At the end of the corridor was a surprisingly ornate door, looking like it might be more at home in a mansion or a palace than the run-down surroundings of the docks.

"It's not what I expected in here," Adam said, taking in the ornate carving on the door and a very expensive looking portrait hanging just off to one side, showing a haughty man, looking down his nose at the world outside the painting.

"It's an interesting story," Lucid told him, "and one which explains a lot about Granny."

"Do we have time for stories?" Adam asked, although he had to admit he was intrigued, despite his keenness to meet the mysterious 'Granny' and see if she was able to help them.

"I think it's a tale worth hearing before you meet her," Lucid told him, with a sparkle in his eyes that suggested he was as keen to tell the story as Adam was to hear it. "They say that back when Granny was starting out down here in the docks, she crossed paths with the Right Honourable Donald Fitzroy. He is the superior looking chap you might have spotted in the portrait. He had an interest in a number of businesses in this area, and one day when he was visiting he bumped into Granny, although that wasn't the name she went by back then. She was begging on the streets at the time, scraping together the first few threads that started her on her way."

"What was she called then?" Adam asked, "I presume that she still had a name."

"She probably did," Lucid replied, "but nobody knows it now. She is just 'Granny' to friend and enemy alike. No one asks, and I would encourage you to show the same discretion. Anyway… he mocked her in the street, showing off to one of his business associates. They say he kicked over her collection plate, called her a few rude names and then didn't think anything more about it… or her."

Adam raised his eyebrows, "and…?"

"He owned a huge manor house just outside of Nocturne," Lucid continued, with a gesture taking in the surrounding corridor and the opulent decoration. "Years later, when Granny had established herself down in the docks she went after Fitzroy. While he hadn't given her a second thought, I understand that she had thought about him, and that moment back down on the streets, quite a lot. She took him for everything he had. He lost his businesses, one after another, and eventually his home. She stripped everything of value from his Manor House and had it shipped down to the docks, used it to decorate her offices. It serves as a reminder, you don't cross Granny, she doesn't forgive and she doesn't forget... ever."

His story complete, Lucid knocked politely on the heavy wooden door and then stood waiting, head tilted to one side, listening intently. A few minutes passed silently, and when Adam went to step forward, Lucid raised a warning finger to him and mouthed the word 'wait' to him. A further long and increasingly boring minute ticked away and then a small bell, that Adam had failed to see hidden away in a shadowy corner of the ceiling, jangled quietly.

Nodding to himself Lucid pushed the heavy wooden door open, which to Adams secret disappointment didn't creak or make any sort of ominous noise at all.

Despite this rather ordinary entrance, the rest of the room that Adam and Lucid walked into was far more interesting. Although large and well-furnished, the massive amount of clutter made it immediately feel much smaller and slightly cramped. The centre of the room was dominated by a large and intricately carved desk, with a heavy weaved rug directly in front of it. However, the rest of the space around this was a chaotic mess of heaped trinkets, ornaments, and other expensive looking knick-knacks. They were piled high on every available surface, with a cluster of fine china vases on the nearest table teetering precariously, squeezed into so little space that Adam was convinced breathing too heavily could cause them to topple and crash to the ground.

Behind the desk was a diminutive old woman, who Adam assumed must be Granny. A face like a slightly rotten apple, wrinkled and brown, stared intently at Adam, the gaze so piercing that he had to look away. When he looked back she had turned her attention away from him and onto Lucid, standing slowly and holding out a hand to him across the desk. Her clothing was faded but expensive looking, a mixture of velvets and lace shrouding her in shapeless, opulent layers.

"So, what do you want from Granny youngster?" Granny asked, her voice a strange mixture of accents that Adam couldn't fully place. The edges of her accent rang with the tuneful melodies of the Sornette's lilting speech, but this was balanced by a much harsher undertone that ran through everything she said, like strands of barbed wire concealed within a harmless looking hedgerow.

"Well… you see we were hoping you could help us find someone…" Adam began, before being interrupted by Granny's rasping laugh.

"Heh… I didn't mean you stripling," she said, "I was talking to your tall friend here." With which she turned her attention back to Lucid, her arm still outstretched.

Lucid lowered his head, planting a kiss on the back of the wrinkled, claw-like hand before straightening up again. Apparently satisfied with this, Granny lowered herself back into her chair with an audible groan of effort.

"So?" she asked him.

"My young companion is correct," Lucid told her. "We are looking for someone, someone with very specific experience. In particular we need a captain, someone who knows their way around the Dwam, someone who has sailed the sea of dreams." He paused as if expecting some sort of reaction from Granny, but she said nothing. Instead, she just sat there looking across at Lucid with a calculating expression on her face.

"You know everything that takes place in the docks," Lucid continued. "Every ship, every trader and every captain that passes through Nocturne. If anyone would know who could undertake a voyage on the Dwam it would be you."

Granny continued to look back at Lucid without speaking, but Adam could see the cogs in her head turning, and after a moment she spoke.

"I presume that this child is the reason you are here?" she asked, pointing to Adam. "An unusual journey for one so young to be undertaking." She turned her attention back to Adam for a moment, beckoning for him to approach with one gnarled finger.

Rather hesitantly Adam walked across to stand in front of her, caught in the glare of the lamps hanging around the desk and the small oasis of clear space that surrounded it. Up close Granny was even more ancient than Adam had first thought and considerably grubbier. The fine clothes didn't appear to have been washed for some time and there was an unpleasant smell that he tried not to react to.

"It's a very rare thing you're asking for," she began. "There are only two captains that I would trust on the Dwam, and unfortunately for you, one of them is quite mad."

"So, who is the other one?" Adam asked. She smiled back at him, not particularly pleasantly, revealing what remained of her teeth. A series of alternating black and brown tombstones in remembrance of long lost and sadly missed oral hygiene. "Oh my..." she giggled, "...you don't understand at all do you? It's the mad one that you need to find. The other one is much, much worse."

"Where then, where do we find this captain?" Adam asked her, trying not to breathe in too heavily, her last exhalation having made him slightly woozy.

At his question she held out a wrinkled hand, the skin on her fingers hanging loose, like oversize jumpers on skinny children, waiting to grow into their clothes. Despite her lack of words, her intention was transparent enough.

"Lucid?" Adam turned to his friend, aware that he had no money of his own. Lucid sighed, gave a shrug and pulled a small velvet bag from his inside pocket. Holding it between the tips of two long, delicate fingers he dropped it into the grasping claw below.

Without even stopping to check the content of the bag, the hand snapped closed and the bag was stashed below the table. "That will do," she said, "as a down-payment. I will be sure to be in touch when it's time for you to... fully repay me for this favour."

Adam looked across at Lucid, there was still a smile on his face, but to Adam it looked slightly more brittle than it had before and perhaps there was even a spark of anger in his eyes for a split second. Then he managed to control whatever momentary emotion had reared its head and his expression returned to one of bland indifference.

"Your lanky Sornette friend will know where she is," Granny continued, a smile returning to her thin blue lips. "There is a great gathering of his people just over a day's travel from here, a Grand Assembly... you will find her there."

"How do you know?" Lucid said, his expression remaining carefully neutral, the only sign of his doubt being a slightly raised eyebrow. "How do you know that she is at the Assembly?"

"She's desperate for money," she replied, still smiling her unpleasantly toothy smile. "I have heard from my various... contacts at the docks that she is out of funds and her ship is still in for repair. She has been banned from every bank, money lender and gaming house in the city, but there is always a game to be played and prizes to be won at the Grand Assembly... isn't that right?" The last comment was aimed at Lucid, who nodded slightly before remembering himself and pausing rather awkwardly mid-nod.

"Thank you for your time," Lucid said, tapping Adam on the shoulder, giving him notice that their audience was at an end. He nodded again, almost deeply enough to class as a bow, in the direction of the wizened old woman and then pulled open the door, ushering Adam out with him.

As the door closed slowly behind them Adam saw Lucid release a deep exhalation and with it he seemed to deflate slightly.

The confident façade from the meeting with Granny leaving him along with his breath.

"See you later Mr. Lucid," rumbled Carter as they ducked past his huge frame on the way back out into the docks. "Look after yerself."

"I will Carter, you take care too," Lucid replied. Then he grasped Adam's elbow, leading him away and trying to stop him from so obviously gawping. As they weaved their way back through the maze of old warehouses. Lucid was walking faster than normal, with an unfamiliar tightness in his movements, like an overwound clockwork toy, meaning that Adam was forced into an awkward half-run to keep up.

Carter watched them go, intrigued by the curious pairing. He couldn't work out why Lucid would be wandering around the docks with a human. A small, scrawny one at that. Then he shrugged to himself, working things out was something he generally left to Granny. He was so caught up in his thoughts that he didn't notice the patch of dark shadow growing slowly on the wall behind him. It started out as small and innocuous as a single oily raindrop, slowly growing till it was a big as a plate, then again until it was nearly as big as Carter himself.

It was only when it was so big that it nearly filled the wall behind him that Carter become aware of it, an uncomfortable warning sensation itching at the back of his head, and by then it was much, much too late.

BOOKS IN THIS SERIES

The Daydreamer Chronicles
Join Adam and his companions as they fight to save both worlds from the schemes of the Nightmares

The Boy Who Dreamt The World

You would think being able to control your dreams would be fun. But in a place where those dreams can take on a life of their own and nightmares stalk the streets, just making it through the night is hard enough.

There are two worlds that have always lived peacefully alongside each other, the world we know and the Dreamworld, Reverie. Adam's life is turned upside down when he discovers that, as a Daydreamer, he can travel between the two and achieve impossible things. But nothing in the Dreamworld is as straightforward as it looks. There is something new threatening to pull the two worlds apart and Adam and his newly discovered friends are the only ones who can stop it.

As if having to save the world wasn't already hard enough, there are detentions to avoid, a mystery surrounding the odd new girl in his class to solve, and the fact that Adam has absolutely no idea how to control his newly found powers.

'The Boy Who Dreamt the World' is the first book in the Daydreamer Chronicles series.

Where Dreams End

Finally, Adam has found where his mum could be hidden....
She is somewhere deep within the Dream World of Reverie, but getting to her won't be easy.

For a start she is somewhere far on the other side of the world, a place where no sane person would ever choose to go, the place the Nightmares come from. Even worse than that, the Queen of the Nightmares has her own plans in place, and Adam is caught right in the middle of her schemes.

Then there is the small matter of a war between Nightmare factions, an impossible voyage across the great sea of dreams and clashes with the most ancient beings in all of Reverie.

Fortunately for Adam he has the help of an even odder group of friends than usual, which in Reverie means very odd indeed. But even with the help of friendly dream beings, Nightmare freedom fighters and clockwork cyborgs, this time Adam is in real trouble, stuck in the place where dreams end.

'Where Dreams End' is the third book in the Daydreamer Chronicles series.

Frozen Dreams

Adam thought he had won. The Queen of the Nightmares defeated and Reverie made safe; but he was wrong and now the Dream World is in greater danger than ever, with enemies both old and new threatening him from every side.

The best chance of saving the Stairway of Dreams could lie within Adam's pendant, and the only person able to unlock those secrets lives deep in the icy homeland of the Drőmer.

It's a cold and inhospitable wasteland, and the only thing Adam and his friends are guaranteed is a frosty reception. To make matters worse there is a mysterious new Daydreamer in Reverie and only time will tell if they're a friend or foe.

'Frozen Dreams' is the fourth book in the Daydreamer Chronicles series.

Tales From Reverie: Maya

This is a Novella length tale, giving a brand new perspective on the events in the first three books, especially if you ever wondered whatever happened to Maya.

Something bad is coming...
All Maya wanted was a new life, far away from the barren plains of the west. Unfortunately for her what she got was something very different and now she works for the 'Five', the self-proclaimed protectors of Reverie.

There are rumours of a new Horror forming on the fringes of the Dreamworld, and what was supposed to be just another mission is already turning out to be much worse than Maya could ever have expected, with the future of the entire world hanging in the balance.

Before Adam's adventures in Reverie ever began there was another hero fighting to protect the world from Nightmares. See the events of the Daydreamer Chronicles unfold from a completely different perspective.

No Daydreams, no powers, but a whole lot of trouble.

Printed in Great Britain
by Amazon

62943932R00113